Mada

A Novel by
Kleya Forté-Escamilla

Sister Vision
Black Women and Women of Colour Press
P.O. Box 217, Station E
Toronto, Ontario
Canada M6H 4E2

ISBN 0-920813-69-0
Copyright © 1993 Kleya Forté-Escamilla
All rights reserved. No part of this book may be reproduced or transmitted in any form or by any means without permission in writing from the publisher except in the case of reviews.

Canadian Cataloguing in Publication Data
Escamilla, Kleya Forté-
Mada
ISBN 0-920813-69-0
1. Mada
PS3555.S27M34   1993   813'.54   C93-094273-6

This world is but one sweet moment

*A*CKNOWLEDGEMENTS

My sincere thanks to Sister Vision Press, the women who worked to publish this book and also liked the story; and with deep appreciation to those who affected my life so profoundly during my years in California.

To my first friends, Barbara, Mary, Connie, Joanna, Lynnie and Beanie, and the times of hope and promise.

To Josette and the Mondanaros for all the spaghetti and love I've eaten at your house;

To the writing group Quelites, especially Gloria, Magdalena, Megan and Carmen, for that brief season of recognition and support — truth and beauty are forever;

To Nicolette, Carol, Kathy and Tillie, for your encouragement of my writing at a time when I could have gone either way. To all others who through love, friendship, or adversity have made me stronger than I ever thought I could be.

And especially to Gisela for showing me the heart of the German people.

This book is for all of you, with love.

Kleya

CHAPTER 1

THE DAY MADA CAME BACK INTO MY WORLD, I BEGAN to awaken. The way we met, the way we loved — nothing could stop me. I floated towards her out of my quiet stream, and cast myself from unthinkable heights into that raging river. And it didn't drown me. It didn't wreck my soul but brought me wind-struck and bright to my own shore.

It was a quiet night in the Purple Rose and I was tired of texts that wouldn't yield, of the small minds that confine institutions. The winter was dirty and damp with the flat heavy presence of the sea. Thick fog came off the coast and turned into cold drizzling rain. I longed for the clean frozen lands of home, for the sight of geese flying above the green pines in a red flush of sky. I wanted to walk on the reserves with the only sound the whispering voice of snowflakes speaking with the spirits of trees, but the Great Lakes were far away.

I wanted to be free for one night, anonymous even to myself. At the Purple Rose I was among friends. I could stretch out my legs and look at the women at the bar. I sat in the dark in my corner and watched the faces, lips and eyes, the beautiful hands and breasts of women. I didn't want anything and it felt good.

There were a few straight men around that night, maybe the ones who want a dyke to beat them. It wasn't what I wanted, but sometimes I liked the company of older men who could converse intelligently and keep their hands to themselves, so when he came over to my table I didn't say no.

The accent was German when he asked what I was drinking. He didn't raise his eyebrows when I said "Perrier." And he didn't insist when I declined, showing him my still-full glass. He was dressed to meet GQ standards. Designer suit, elegantly lightweight, cashmere overcoat with an Italian silk tie. He didn't ask me right away what I did, what my name was, or where I came from. I liked that. We talked about the fog and the small-town feeling of this coastal city so near Silicon Valley, about the healing effect of the place and its people.

He surprised me. "Midwest. North more recently. Arizona?"

"Great Lakes, eastern Arizona," I said. "How did you know?"

"The design of your ring. Pima, isn't it? Latina and what else?"

"A mixture," I said flatly.

"No matter."

I looked down and noticed my Wellingtons were almost touching his Van Dykes. They were the best, but people pick certain shoes for reasons not always apparent.

It was his turn to be surprised when I said, "Why were you in the southwest?"

His face changed colour for just a moment.

"Forget it," I said.

"It's all right. I was there with my wife." The silk cuffs at his wrist shone in the bar light. There were beads of sweat on his upper lip and below his precisely-trimmed sideburns.

"I think she will like you very much."

"What do you mean? My people? Or does she like lesbians?"

"Both."

I laughed, but he was serious. "Would you like to meet her?" Before I could reply he added, "You're not like the others. You're a thinker."

"I read some books. I learned a little. Now I'm trying very hard to forget it."

"That's very different from someone who's never thought at all."

I didn't like where this was going. I hate people who can get into the smart place in me because they think they can flatter me that way.

"I know some beautiful women who would disagree."

He ignored that. "You're looking for something other than the merely conventional?"

"That word covers a lot of ground. But yes, not everything has been felt."

"Of course."

"Why isn't your wife here?" We both knew he had me then, but he said evenly, "She travels a lot. And tonight there were others to consider. But I know she'll be glad to see you."

"Where?"

"Not far. It's a wonderful place." He said it like he meant it.

He told me about the mountains and the wilderness, and I realized he was talking for her. But I had already made up my mind. I was already feeling the softness of her gown, moving aside its folds with my fingers.

I don't know what kind of car I'd imagined, but it was a handsome old English Riley. As the fine old sportster moved smoothly through the darkness, places I knew became strange to me. I looked out at the wet pavement and later at the redwoods that towered over us as we drove towards the summit. Then we turned off on a secondary road that looked private, drove around some curves and through a security gate, then down a long driveway.

The house sat below the road in a clearing. I couldn't see any light or tell the size or shape of the house until we were right up on it. The entrance hall was as big as the living room in many of the houses I knew. There was a fountain with running water and indigo tiles and a tree reaching for a peaked skylight. Then we were walking across a vast beautiful rug into a split-level room.

There was no furniture, just pillows in front of a Swedish fireplace and a glass table on the other side, near some French doors. After pouring me the promised glass of Perrier, he told me to relax and disappeared. I stood by the fire and it was glorious. I found a washroom and used it. After a while, I roamed around the room a bit. We had taken off our shoes at the door and now I felt like I was walking in a huge sunken bath, ankle-deep with fleece.

The French doors were slightly open now. I didn't hear anything, so I went up to them. They opened on to another room, where a fire burned in a big rough, stone fireplace against the wall. There were pillows and more white fleece covered the floor.

She was standing there, barefoot, as though she had been going somewhere and had just stopped to watch the fire. There was an expression on her face I couldn't read. She knew I was there but didn't turn towards me. She sighed and sat down. I sat too, my legs suddenly weak at the sight of her. I didn't need to look twice to make sure. I knew her. We sat side by side looking at the fire.

"It's compelling, isn't it?" she said, gesturing at the fire. She spoke with a slight German accent and a very British delivery. But I already knew what her voice sounded like. I knew it from the recording I had worn out long ago, a magnificent voice saying, "I am in your power . . . subject to your will and your demands. A slave, a slave then! No, I cannot endure the thought of that! Never!"

Mada

Mada von Brecht as Ibsen's Hedda. As an undergraduate I had spent most of my spare time alone, hiding in the Record Room, listening to her voice. I knew every detail of the picture on the cover of the album: the beauty of that unusual head, the full black hair, the lowered thick-lashed eyes, the expressive hands placed alongside her cheek in the old style of portraiture. Now her hair was cut short, combed straight back, emphasising the jaw — too strong for any other woman — the cleft chin, the mouth wide and mobile.

Then in her mid thirties, she was the darling of the Theatre Arts Department; we spent a whole year's performance budget to bring her one Spring. I went to all three performances, sitting close enough to hear her breathe, to see every movement of her body, hear every nuance in her voice. On the last night everyone went backstage. I stood back, watching them crowd around her, waiting for a chance to ask her to sign my album cover, trying to smile and look unafraid.

I couldn't take my eyes off her. I watched her talk to each person, study each intently, then lift the hair of a beautiful young woman, letting it fall slowly from her fingers. And I ran, afraid of what she would see in my eyes, afraid of what I might see in hers and the pain I couldn't hide. I retreated down the stairs, clutching my album to my breast, overwhelmed by desire and fear.

The fire was beginning to burn low, so I got up, took some oak from the basket, picked up the poker and started building up the fire. It was wonderful to feel so warm on

Mada

that foggy winter night. The dampness was something I could never get used to. I moved the embers around. I stacked and stoked and raised a strong fire. Yellow, blue and green sparks danced as I turned back to her, her incredible eyes filled with green sparks like the flames. I looked at her too. I had to. Then she got up and moved to secure the doors. I sat back and remembered the rest.

I had grown up, dropped out of graduate school. I travelled and got older, left the Midwest and came to California where I heard there were women like me. I came out, painfully, and broke away from that first woman, also painfully. I lived for a while in the Southwest, travelled, came back to San Francisco for three years and eventually made my way down the coast to this small town by the sea to finish my education. Two years had gone by. But when I was in San Francisco something happened.

My memories of the time are intense, confusing. Experiments with the drugs of the day made everything soul-wrenching and extreme. But one time would always be clear in my head: the night I heard Mada's name again.

There was a woman in the building I lived in, Midge, a photographer. Shy. Very lonely and very calm. The kind of calm I learned could appear cold, but hide a passionate interior. Cool, long fingers. I wanted to know her better and one afternoon went looking for her. Her brother Jake told me where to find her. Mada von Brecht came to Sausalito every few months, he said. And she would call Midge. Midge would drive over to Mada's hotel room and not come back for two or three days. Then Midge went back to her mother's house on Nob Hill. "Couldn't take the life anymore," Jake said.

A lot happened after that. Wilder, more personal adventures took over my life, but in the end I left San Francisco without fulfilling my dreams. Now Mada was here, close enough for me to hear her breathe.

There was the soft rustle of draperies sliding into place. I smelled her scent as she lay down beside me, sensed the fullness I had sensed around him. Until that moment I hadn't once thought about how I got there or what it might mean. I didn't care. Tomorrow, when I would again be struggling with my dissertation in a tiny cold office, was so far away it didn't even exist.

I felt her fingers on my bare wrist, cool on my warm skin. Her touch was so light that I felt the hairs on my arm rise and fall in the wake of her fingers. Then she lifted my hand and brushed it over the rise of her hipbone and onto the bare skin of her thigh.

My fingers began to move of their own accord, but her hand stayed on mine, guiding me, making me feel what she felt. She felt me tremble and I felt her pleasure by the slight quiver of her fingers on the back of my hand. When I heard her voice, I knew she felt me loving her and that was what I wanted — to adore her. Had she looked at me again with those fantastic eyes, I don't think I could have stood it. But her eyes were closed as she lay on top of me and kissed my throat, her lips as soft as her fingers. She moved my hands back to her hips and pushed them down.

Mada

My mouth followed the traces of my fingers; she smelled like the sea and when she began to move, the wave flowed over me. My regrets and losses were nothing. Later I felt her mouth move slowly over my breast, her tongue like a butterfly tasting the surface of a leaf. I took her in my arms and nearly wept at her wide-open eyes, her face offered without reserve, without compromise, making her all the more desirable. She let me gaze at her, then knelt and kissed me once on the forehead and once on the cheek. I felt the shape of her mouth and saw her lashes shining in the firelight as she lifted away from me. But my eyes closed again and I forgot to ask her why.

The Beowulf seminar met on the next afternoon in the attic of the old library building. As I spoke, I faced a beautiful clerestory window, covering most of the west wall and offering a view of the campus below. The pasture of the old ranch rolled away from me, ending in pines spread before the winds rushing in from the sea. I sensed the waves crashing and phantom sea mist stung me. But Old English poetics, the sounds and meanings I'd found so intriguing, slipped away, and I found myself staring at the ancient text without understanding. Mada von Brecht beckoned to me from fragments of firelight. The touch of skin and lips and flashes of body memory came and went, leaving me shaking.

Graduate students sprawled around the long table. My presentation sounded intelligent enough. The old language rolled easily from my mouth. But somewhere in the mists of a half-formed world, I was looking at a maroon scarf lying across my jacket. She had covered me and placed several items beside me. The scarf on top, beneath it a sweater, silk underwear, then a hundred-dollar bill. The house was empty. The fire still burned — she must have put on more wood. The Riley was gone from in front the house.

The cab had come. I'd paid for the trip back to town and put the change down on the clothing she'd left. At the last minute, I took the scarf and in its place left my office number. A perk I got for working on my doctorate, the office was a hole in the wall, really, but it had a phone and most of the time I was there.

After I left, I realized she didn't know my name. I didn't know if I wanted her to.

Winter passed as winters do here, with persistent cold rains that feed the redwoods but make it hard for my VW to start in the mornings. The holidays came and I went home to the solitude of the North. I spent Christmas day tramping over the reserves. I walked beside streams that had burst through the ice to reveal blue-black waters tumbling briefly over the rocks before disappearing in the icy course. I ran across the frozen fields and once fell hard as I tried to assault a small hill without slowing down. It knocked the breath out of me. As I gasped for air, I felt another pain — her absence.

Later, as the colourless day closed in fiery reds and a deep, lingering orange behind the black wings of geese, I cried. I couldn't push it aside any longer. I had to see her.

CHAPTER 2

WHEN I CAME BACK TO CALIFORNIA MY HEAD WAS clear, and in spite of the aching in my heart, I felt rested. Gradually, I returned to my work. Except for a few visits to the Purple Rose, where I never stayed long, I hardly left my office. But one night after a dry spell, it rained again, a warm, wet rain that signals the coming of spring. I drove to the mountains, coaxing my VW up to the summit and getting lost in the roads at the top. The windshield wipers moved too slowly, and I could barely see out the small window. I passed one road after another, watching the headlights on the muddy dirt road, but I couldn't find the house. I don't think I expected to. And if I had, I didn't expect to find her. And I would never have gone up to the door. It was just that I had to think about her, had to let myself know it was all right.

Mada

When I got back to town I slept. That night I dreamed about her for the first time. I awakened at 5:00 a.m., chasing dissolving images. Excitement and sorrow faded from my body with the first grey light. The morning was cloudy and cold and my office was an icebox. I stood in front of the electric heater to warm my hands, then tossed my jacket into a heap in the corner and sat at my desk.

The poem fragments I was deciphering began to give way, layer by layer. Throughout the day I was exhausted and jubilant by turns. When it got too dark to see, I stopped and stretched painful muscles. The phone rang. I'd been alone all day and I felt exhilarated by my progress — it had been a real breakthrough — and the intrusion irritated me. It took me a while to track down the cord under a mess of papers and clothes, so I barked into the receiver. The voice on the other end laughed.

"Raquel, miene liebe, you must stop working now and come to me!"

"Where are you?" I managed to get out. I didn't ask how she knew my name.

"Oh, very near," she said. "Avery Hall."

Avery Hall? "What are you doing there?"

"Oh, don't worry. I'm well occupied."

I shelved the discs I'd been working on and shut down the computer. I grabbed the maroon scarf and wrapped it around my neck, then drove the VW, its cold engine sputtering and complaining, out of the parking lot and up the hill to Avery. I didn't want to see her. I was crazy to see her. I didn't want to love her so much, didn't want to want her so much. But remembering how it was, I ran towards the building, stopping at the door to catch my breath.

There were a few students sleeping in big armchairs in the lounge and a small knot of women over to the side making a lot of noise. They were young, bright-looking and singing the words to a popular rock song. She was deep in conversation with a blind man who was tapping his hand in time to something she was saying. She wore dark glasses, but I knew the smiling mouth, the tilt of the head and intensity of her body. She turned towards me. Even behind the dark glasses, her eyes captured me. She took off the glasses and waved me over to her. Turning back to the man, she grasped his hands in hers, then got up swiftly and walked to meet me.

I felt awkward, but she held me tightly and then stepped back to let me talk.

"What are you doing here? How did you know I was here?"

"I made enquiries. Discreetly, of course. David told me."

"You mean David Ingersow?"

"Yes. He's a very old friend." When we were in her car, she asked, "When do you have to be back?"

"I teach a class on Tuesday morning."

"Fine. Good."

She wasn't dressed for the cold evening. I took the scarf and put it around her neck, tucking the ends inside the collar of her suit. We drove in silence up the coast on

Highway 1. When the car was warm she handed the scarf back. "This is all you took."

It wasn't a question, but I felt she wanted me to answer. Nothing fit. I thought about it and she didn't try to hurry me.

"I couldn't . . . demean my actions. But I didn't want to forget you too soon."

We drove on in silence, the Mercedes taking the long steep grades easily, the sea breaking below us in the darkness. She reached out and stroked my cheek. I took her hand, bringing her fingers to my mouth. After that the tension eased and the car floated up the highway.

I think I knew then that I would go anywhere, do anything, be anything she wanted.

"Oh? Are you so good at forgetting?"

"No. Are you?"

"The way you came to me," she said, "makes me ask the same questions. But you see, we can never really know what's true."

"You're the first," I said, "in a long time."

"And if I said that too, would you believe it?"

She didn't wait for my answer. "You think love exists only according to a precise recipe. But what if love's only purpose is to celebrate, to eclipse the sorrow of life?"

"Don't you want more?"

"In the beginning loving and caring are free. Why should I want to limit that with imperfections?"

"I'm not like you. With time I expect good things."

"You want to make love pay the price for knowledge.

If you understand what I'm saying, then you know that love is also cruel."

"We are imperfect and we still feel love. And anyway, that's not love you're talking about. It's sex, the act of sex."

"Sex? No, my darling. Only lust has no memory. Do you think I'd throw away the tenderness? The caring? Even to be a good lover it takes more than just desire."

I wanted to tell her about the album cover, that I had loved her for a long time, that we weren't so young anymore, but I was in turmoil and could only stare out the window, thinking bizarre thoughts.

Her voice was affectionate and warm. "Don't you want to know where we're going? I'm taking you to my home."

I knew she wanted it to be okay between us. I wanted that too. "I thought that other place was your home."

"It's another part of my life. It was by accident that you went there."

We had turned off the main highway on to Route 2 but were still going north over the hills. She suddenly swung off, on to a two-lane dirt road. The woods got thicker on each side. Tall eucalyptus flourished every few feet. She slowed down and opened her window. "I'm sorry for the cold air, but I can never find the entrance. Ah, here it is!"

There was no place for mail, only a *New York Times* box and a sign saying PRIVATE ROAD. She hit the gas and we flew around the next three curves. I was just wondering about the paint job on the Mercedes when the road ran out under a large top-heavy pine.

A security light burned on the porch, but she left the headlights on and they spotted the surrounding darkness. Then she turned off the motor and we sat in the dark. I didn't know what to feel, what to think. I reached for her and she came into my arms. The scent between her breasts rushed up into my face. I felt like my heart would break.

"Oh, my dear," she said.

She turned her shining eyes away. "Come. There's a lot to do."

She shoved me gently towards the wood pile and I carried a few armloads into the house while she took care of the utilities. I was standing outside looking up at the sky, letting the shadows rise from my mind with my breath when I heard her.

"You look good here. You belong outside, under the trees." She smiled.

"How long are you staying this time?"

"A month." A whole month!

"I'm preparing a new reading. When I do that I come here. And you? David said you're working on your dissertation?'

"How well do you know him?"

"He's one of my oldest friends in this country."

"Does he know about us?"

"My dear, David and I only ask each other what we know the other wants to tell. Would you care?"

"No," I said truthfully. "Would you?"

"Yes, but not for the reason you might think."

She quickly asked me about my work, and I began to tell her about it as we slowly walked along the edge of the woods. We gradually stopped talking. I felt so natural with her, like I'd come home for the weekend. Then I burst out laughing. "I don't have anything with me again," I explained.

"It's not necessary. I wouldn't bring you here without taking care of your needs," she said. She was so sure of herself and so matter-of-fact. I hadn't heard from her in months and then she tells me she's prepared for me?

"You'd better make it disposable," I said.

"Often I'm travelling. Here and in Europe. Much of the time I'm surrounded by people I need something from. When I can make myself available to someone — for myself, like now — it's very special to me."

I was glad for her words, but I was also hurt and exasperated.

"Hey!" I caught up to her. Her eyes were almost level with mine.

"It's all right. Really!" We walked back to the house.

I stood forever under a shower, steaming myself inside and out. And I found a thick terry robe, maroon, like the scarf. One of my favourite colours.

I stoked the fire and lay down on the tatami beside her. Tiny hairs, still wet from the tub she'd been in, curled at her temples. As I revelled in looking at her, I thought about the old language, about the study of meaning. Poetry, art, drama — all were trying to say what we really mean, what we know about reality, about truth. But she had said there was no truth.

Her eyes were open and staring at the fire. She began to talk.

The words came one at a time, unrelated. She took me back to the Allied fire-bombing of Dresden during the Second World War, to the woman she might have been and the woman she was because of it.

"The flames took all that I, a young girl, wanted to protect. What remained were deliberate offenses against innocence. As we picked up the bricks, I examined them one by one . . . and I saw the holes we fall through. We were looking for what we'd known in the rubble, but it was no more. I had to give new meanings to old words. New feelings leapt up, pure as flame." Her fingers hurt me, but I didn't pull away.

"When we made a home — the first one — I read to them, to the other women, for the first time. They listened to me as if they were listening to God." With my free hand I stroked her hair over and over, gently soothing her.

"You think I should sleep," she whispered. "Safely, safely, always knowing what tomorrow will bring, but you're wrong."

I stroked her hair. "I don't know what I think anymore."

She relaxed little by little. I heard the windchimes and the trees moving in answer to the restlessness of the wind. The firelight flickered on the shoji screens, illuminating a single fine Japanese vase on a small cedar table.

Nothing was what I had expected, but everything around her was right. I wanted to kiss her but couldn't. She moved away from me then and said my name, but I still couldn't move. Her eyes were wet.

"Mada," I said. "I'm here." I needed her to want me — not just when she had looked for me, got the clothes, found me and brought me here — but right now.

"Why don't you do what you're dying to do?"

Then I reached out to her and she took me hungrily. The fire raged out of her green eyes into mine. She held me pressed against the floor, her hair falling over her face while tears made tracks down the sides of her mouth. I reached up to her, but she rolled away from me.

I felt her hands, slow and measured, removing my robe. I was desperate with wanting her. Tenderly touching my breasts and kissing where her fingers had been, she understood my wanting better than I did. She took it and used it to sharpen my pleasure, holding me so I couldn't move, couldn't turn from her touch.

Holding my hips with her strong hands, she focused our desire on that one place until it swelled to bursting beneath her tongue and her teeth, moving her wonderful body so I could reach her with my mouth. With her first cry, I began to explode and we plunged together to the bottom of the spiral.

Then, in the vulnerable moments that followed, I brought her to me and reached deep inside her. She gripped my arms hard, and as I moved her, she began to cry out. I held her securely as she moved and shuddered against me, then turned her over and lay on top of her, pressing myself to her ass, kissing the beautiful line of her back, moving aside the hair that lay wet against her neck. Covering her, I lay beside her, filled with her loveliness and her pleasure. We rested. She tempted me again and satisfied me again with the same sweet, powerful passion.

Afterwards, bodiless and high, I walked deeper into myself. I became aware that my linguistic studies actually concerned states of being, unrestricted by time and place. And the ground I was beginning to explore was in a world still being created, inside words that held many meanings. My body was woman, beast and natural world. I looked into the darkness and it blinded me. When I opened my eyes, I knew I had glimpsed the fire from which she took her brilliance.

I thought about a lot that weekend. She shared her work with me, as if we had always been and would always be together in a country I neither knew nor had ever imagined. We acted with the full knowledge of our mortality: as if we would live forever. The way we made love, what we did to and took from each other, bordered on making extinct everything I thought was real: my personality, my identity as a lesbian, all I had fashioned to contain and limit myself.

I was moved to a tenderness and a sense of loss I'd never felt before. I thought I would never love this much again, never feel such wholeness and such anguish.

I left before she asked me to go, like I had acted each day with her — without naming and with certainty. There was nothing I could ask that she hadn't already given. Yet I wanted to ask.

To agree each time, she said, was what she could offer. It was her nature to burn and I could only warm myself at her fire. I couldn't be like her. I couldn't explain her. But I needed to explain to myself how we could turn each other inside out then walk away without defining the future. I wanted to rip this love apart, shred it to death with explanations, justify to myself the actions of someone who didn't know the meaning of the word.

CHAPTER 3

WHEN I SAW HER AGAIN IT WAS SUMMER AND freezing as only San Francisco summers can. I had finished what I came to California to do, but I lingered, exploring the possibility of teaching in a private school, looking for work that might give me time for my own research. I was used to a spartan life. It had come easy after the *nouveau* opulence of my immigrant parents who had achieved the American dream, a dream they — especially my Latino father — had forced on me when I was growing up.

I was enjoying a few days in Stinsen Beach with some easy-going women, all of us guests of our friend, Susan. We were indulging ourselves with harmless flirting and long carefree days and nights of beach fun. Then I went to meet her.

San Francisco. The city still confused me as soon as I

Mada

entered that long, dreamlike one-way descent into downtown at three in the morning. Too many memories looked back from the pale facades of those old Victorian buildings. I took it in — faces like damaged lands, ruins of the past.

She was in an older pensione in a quiet section of Powell Street, elegant without pretension, furnished with antiques that accommodated as well as being lovely to look at. It was easy to be there. And she got past the shell I used to touch the outside world. I wanted her to. She was the way she always was: careful, exciting, taking her eyes away only to fall deeper into me with the next glance. And I was crazy in love, enough to erase our separation in an instant, enough to find her arms and surrender to an abandoned pleasure in her, to touch and be touched.

The second evening, I made us go out. The fog had retreated for the moment and the moon was bright, friendly and encouraging. I drove to Sausalito.

As we drove over the Golden Gate, the wind came up. Each stanchion came at us out of swirling fog; tall, simply sculpted and beautiful, suggesting mystery and ciphers with no code. We came off the bridge down into cove-like Sausalito. Houseboats bobbed gently and night lights shone peacefully. There were no signs, no neon. Even the bar where we went for the best Irish coffee in the Bay had no sign, just a heavy stained-glass front door. It was a private place, right for quiet sharing. She took Courvoisier. And I started to talk about Midge.

Maybe I was casting for an anchor to hold her to me,

but I didn't know it then. Once I decided, I didn't waste any time.

"Mada, I know Midge."

She hesitated. "Yes." Then her eyes misted, or maybe I couldn't see her very well. I was incredulous. "You know, Mada?"

"She talked to me about you."

"Why?"

"She was very attracted to you."

I took this in and told her I'd been attracted to Midge. It was more than that, I tried to explain.

"But you wouldn't be with her?"

"I couldn't. The first time with a woman had . . . hurt me. And then with Midge, it felt as if it could be a rushing tunnel to . . . a place that would break me. I would be light, but I would be disassembled, and I didn't know if I could survive, as myself. I was frightened, and I waited. And later, it was too late."

Mada let her breath out. "In all this time, you've never tried to see her?" Her question hung in the air as I groped for the answer. I didn't know what she knew or didn't know about the way things ended for me in San Francisco, but I said, "I purposefully allowed the academic world to cover me completely. I didn't want to know about Art, about photographers, about artists. It was safer that way, and for a long time, I convinced myself it was enough. It was easy to let time slide."

Mada inhaled, moving the brandy sniffer around and around in her hands. Then she stood up.

Mada

"We have to leave." I looked at her in confusion. "I have to be alone with you," she said.

I followed her. She drove this time, taking us into the hills above Sausalito. The view was breathtaking. She pulled off the road. A cold wind had wiped out the fog and freed the stars. The fog still sat on the bridge, but across the bay San Francisco breasted the sea with her sparkling lights and below, the blue-black waters of the inlet ran contemplative and silent.

We didn't speak. There was no need to until we were together in a small room of an unassuming hotel at the top of the hill. I accused her, "You knew who I was then, didn't you? That first night when you saw me?"

She didn't answer. Instead she took a photo out of her bag and there we were: me, Midge, her brother Jake and his friend Donny, who lived upstairs. Laughing, loving each other and totally ripped. I couldn't remember who had been the instigator of the image making that night, Midge or Jake? They were both photographers and always seemed to be competing for the same ideas, racing to see who could make formal expression happen first.

"Christ!" I sat down. "What else did she tell you?"

"There was one night — you were very near to her. She couldn't stand it after you left."

I remembered leaning my head, with the long hair I had then, over the back of the chair until I was inches from Midge's hands, feeling her wanting me but never looking in her eyes — too unwilling and unable to admit my own desire. As though holding back gave me power —

Mada

too afraid. Had I known I was punishing her? Had I known and not cared? My dishonesty that night now showed in my voice. "She told you all this?"

"Her fantasies about you were complete. She showed me."

"And you let her? It was all right with you?"

"She was wonderful. She gave me what she wanted to feel with you. And then she cried in my arms."

I wanted to say something but she didn't let me.

"You see, I made love with you long before we met in that house."

"Oh Mada, don't you know?" I had to speak. I had to tell her. "You became real for me because of Midge. She brought you back to me and sometimes I didn't know how to separate you, or even if it was possible!"

She said simply, "I know." And she held me then and kissed me. Now it was her and Midge and me and I felt Midge's long, cool fingers, her exquisite blondness reaching out through Mada, making me admit it all to her.

The next night I left the city alone. At six the following morning Mada flew to Berlin.

Driving away from the city, I manoeuvred jerkily past the marina to the bridge. I looked back once from the marina side, but the city was already lost to the fog. On the mountain road to Stinsen I drove recklessly, grinding gravel on the steep curves winding down to the beach. I reached Susan's house after midnight and ran the car right up on the sand, pulled my sleeping bag out and collapsed in it. The tide was in, waves flapping on the beach a few feet away; the fog a wall I couldn't see beyond.

Mada

The feeling that Mada was drawing farther away from me woke me. I walked, shivering, along the water as far as the rocks and back again. The sun began breaking through, bringing out the bougainvillaea in patches of red and purple around the houses on the cliff.

The weekend guests were gone. My friend had shut herself in her bedroom with her mystery novels, leaving me the run of the house. I tried to think about the work I was doing; the interruption in my life had proven fatal to my schedule. I was trying to read late at night when Susan came out of her bedroom with the phone. I heard the buzz of an overseas connection. Mada was still at the airport in Berlin. She sounded very tired and fragile.

"My dear, Midge is dead."

"What?" I turned hot and cold at the same time.

"No one knew for sure what happened. It looked like an overdose, maybe deliberate . . ."

"When?" She told me it must have occurred soon after I left San Francisco.

"Why didn't you tell me before? The other night?"

She said painfully, "It could serve no purpose, and it would have meant losing my last hours with you."

I strived for an explanation. "She wasn't an addict."

"No."

"If I'd been different . . ."

She spoke kindly. "When a woman decides to die it's very complicated. The final decision is clear and simple in her mind, but getting there is complicated. Others can't imagine and we can't interrupt it that easily."

Mada

A blast of Anne Murray came out of Susan's room suddenly, then stopped.

"Miene liebling, Raquel. Don't be afraid to love."

I held the receiver to my ear a few seconds longer, listening to the dial tone, with that wrenching feeling in my stomach again. Then I carried the phone into Susan's room.

The next morning I floored the gas pedal, crossing the bridge at dawn, stalling at the toll booth. Chilled through, my hair flying in the wind, I drove into Golden Gate Park. In the fog I couldn't tell where I was. I drove around and around. Monterrey pines spread over my head, and in unexpected corners, I suddenly saw gladioluses, their blood-red stalks brazen, and fresh-flowing carpets of begonias, lush and innocent with dew. I came out suddenly at the west entrance to Haight Street.

The streets were almost empty, the sidewalks wet, windows and doors shut. At Masonic Street I turned down to the panhandle and parked. I got out and walked under rows of eucalyptus trees, now uncertain in a once-so-familiar place. Finding a half-dried spot, I sat down but couldn't stay. I drove back to Haight, found a coffee house I didn't know and ordered sassafras tea. I drank a cup slowly, looking through the window, feeling like a fake tourist. Then I walked around the corner to the house on Masonic Street.

New, yellow paint. Custom blinds in the window where there used to be a Madras curtain. I ran up the stairs briskly, before I could think about that last time. Midge had opened the door wide, the way she always did, a warm, eager look on her face, combing back her straw-blond hair with her fingers. I rang the bell to Apartment A and then slumped. Exhaustion and fearful memories weighed me down. I wanted to leave, but the door squeaked open. It was Jake, in rumpled bed clothes but clean shaven and a straight haircut. He stared at me for a minute, then said, "God, Raquel."

"Yeah," I said and walked past him into the hallway. The large mirrored armoire we'd used to hang our coats on was gone, so I wore my jacket into the studio, stepping around standing lights and piles of magazines and photographs. Why had I come here? Jake went out, came back wearing jeans and a sweatshirt, bringing me coffee without my asking, waiting while I drank some.

"Are you here because of the exhibit?" he asked.

I shook my head. "What exhibit? Where?"

"Midge's retrospective. At the Museum of Modern Art."

"No," I said. "I didn't know about it."

"If that's not why you came, then . . ."

"What happened to us, Jake? We always tried to be straight with each other, no matter what happened to other people. We said we'd be honest."

"Everybody fell in love with you, Raquel. But you didn't seem to know — maybe you really didn't know."

"Damn you," I said. "Damn you, Jake."

"Not me. Anyway, it's over."

"No!"

"Yes. Go to the exhibit. It's her last work. Listen, I'll take you."

"No. I don't think I can be with you." We went together anyway.

From the terrace, the city looked fresh and clean. When they opened the doors the only other person waiting turned in the direction of the Thiebeau exhibit. I followed Jake onto the elevator and then off it. As he kept walking, I stopped.

Wall-sized photographs bounced off me from a distance. In the photographs Jake walked on, his head and body like a 3-D cutout across my eyes, sealing out lips: Mada and I, and Midge too.

If only it had really been like that, would Midge still be alive? I stared at the brilliant composites of bodies and attitudes, identities hidden in shadow and stance. But I knew us: Midge moving us, turning us on, putting us face to face with the inevitable until we were planes of light and dark, flowing flesh inside each other yet kept apart by the placement of our hands and heads.

There was Mada's body, like a supple tree: arms floating out, eyes gazing at her feet while branches and leaves sprouted from her shoulders into a canopy above her head. Is that what Midge thought? The final shots were three-foot high faces of the three of us. Our eyes were shadowed. There was also one small, disquieting black and white shot that didn't fit: an ancient dragon, with a large, heart-shaped emerald in one clawed foot. The rich green of the jewel repeated itself in the dragon's eyes — Mada's eyes.

"Why did you run?" Jake was at my shoulder.

"Because we couldn't make it real enough," I said. We stood facing the portrait of Midge, paling before her soft smile and heart-shaped dimples. She made us speak to her and to each other.

"The closer we got, the more elaborate the fantasy became."

"Midge was at Nepenthe that night."

"Yes, but she was with Mada."

"Didn't you know?"

"I thought Midge was joking when she told me she'd changed her mind. Then she said it was what Mada wanted — I didn't have any choice. It was Mada's call all the way. I went away thinking nothing mattered to Mada. The rest of us could stumble over each other, trying to get out of the way. But she always did whatever was easiest for her."

"She hated problems."

"Maybe."

"And that's what Midge became — a problem."

"None of it was real, I tell you." We were mesmerized by Midge's face, begging us for the truth.

"Mada and I never met. Midge and I never made love."

"It's all there," said Jake, gesturing at the photographs.

"I was at Nepenthe, but I never went in. I knew Mada was there and I never went in."

"You were there. And the three of you photographed each other, so you'd never be able to forget."

I turned Jake around, pinned his blue eyes. "Midge made up pictures. She made up stories."

"You made up your life," said Jake. "And now you can't make the pieces fit." He took a step away from me.

"Maybe Mada and Midge had the same fantasy. And me. Only at the end there was nowhere to go with it."

"They made you fit between them. And it was a perfect fit."

"It was Midge's idea."

"That's what you said."

We were walking again. Mada's eyes were everywhere: loving, frightening, mocking, pleading for Midge's ghost.

"The shot of the three of you — stacked on top of each other like living corpses — that was Mada," said Jake, accusing and bitter.

"No, that was never Mada. Flaunting death, terrifying with instinct and will — that was Mada," I said emphatically. "Midge never thought about design. She had ideas, intuited moments, but it took Mada to make a world out of them."

"You know a lot," Jake said.

"Midge told me. She told me everything and then she manipulated us like paper dolls. I went to Nepenthe that night because it was what she wanted."

"It was the only way you could get Mada."

We reached the back wall, turned around, walked faster.

"I thought it was the only way."

Mada

"And then when you saw them together . . ."

"I didn't see anything, damn it. I ran. I just ran."

"But see, it didn't matter." Jake shook his head. "Mada already knew you were camping on the doorstep of her favourite fuck . . . "

"Don't say it!"

". . . and there was only one thing she could do about it: get you for herself."

"It didn't happen that way." I was repeating myself, stomping down the corridor. "I didn't know Midge. I didn't know Mada. We were imagined people in each other's minds."

"Let's start at the beginning," said Jake gently.

"No, let's not," I told Midge's image.

"You and Mada were together the night Midge died."

"I was alone and far away the night she died," I said quietly and closed the elevator door.

I watched the lights go on and off all the way to the basement, came out below ground level, pushing against a gusting wind from the open sea beyond. Forever is what the sea had told me. Forever was only a moment with Mada, a wave melting into the calm of the ocean. I was desperate with longing. All around I saw broken faces, eyes that were Mada's, lips belonging to Midge. But truthfully, the hands were mine: one on Mada's knee, the other reaching for Midge, images left behind in an unopened box of negatives I never knew existed.

Jake was speaking to me again. "You saw these before."

"Never. I only imagined what she was doing, planning, obsessed with."

"You made her want what you wanted."

"I drew graphic pictures. She made it happen."

"And then you denied knowing."

"I thought that would be it — pictures of nothing."

Jake's words slapped me from the rear of the terrace. "You were stupid and insensitive. A coward."

"I came to life for her."

"For Mada, you mean."

"I didn't plan it."

"You planned every minute."

"Jake, I . . ."

"You went to Nepenthe because you knew Mada would be there. And you knew she'd had enough second-hand sex to make her crazy. You knew you'd get what you wanted. And you didn't care about anyone else."

"But I didn't do it."

"Then what made you run, Raquel? Was it because you knew they'd never be happy with just each other again?

Madeleine Tremaine. Midge. That photograph of you — who took it? Was it Mada? After that night? Did I take it and forget about it? Did I see your lips curl up at the corners, your eyes widen in that anticipating, slightly cross-eyed smile at fantasies coming into reach? And Mada — was I following her, designing my moves until the day I could walk into her life, a stranger . . . ?

Mada

Mada had told me, "I made love with you long before we were together in that house." In my mind I asked Mada, When was it? Tell me, because now I can't find my way and I don't know what I'm guilty of. I only know what it feels like to love you.

The sun came out, lighting up the houses and the trees with colours. Up and down the hills of San Francisco, there were grateful birds, and grateful people. But I just wanted to get away from here and never come back. My grief was for nothing: it didn't bring Midge back and it couldn't keep Mada near me. Grief didn't stop the aching loneliness that left me stranded with only tears and pointless desires.

CHAPTER 4

NO LONGER CONSIDERING WORKING IN THE BAY AREA, I went back to my little town on the central coast. The research grants I'd applied for the year before were pending. I began to think again about what to do if one came through. I poured over volumes on the history of Western Europe before and during the Middle Ages. I thought about time as a matrix for geology and national boundaries and how each affected language and thought. I delved into abstruse matters at night, making myself mentally tired enough to sleep.

During the days I pushed myself to ready my small cabin for winter, getting an early start for the first time. There was plenty to do: stacking wood, repairing the roof, clearing away piles of eucalyptus leaves and pine needles, shoring up the creek bank against flood.

My body ached all the time and I still thought about

Mada

Mada more than I wanted to. Sometimes the wanting brought her back to me. Late at night, her spirit energy was so strong around me that I touched myself. Sometimes these moments of solitary passion left me more awake and needing her, but other times she lingered and I could sleep, warm and spent, as if I were against her breast.

One day, on a trip to the university library, I was pleased to run into David Ingersow. He wasn't on my dissertation committee, but he did help women advance their careers and asked nothing in return. Complete with leather patches on the elbows of his wrinkled corduroy jacket, a much-bitten pipe between his teeth and always in need of a haircut, he roamed the campus. His large liquid eyes and his polite, gentle manner belied his skill at finding the patterns in seemingly disparate facts and at finding the meaning in those patterns. He was a historian who understood philosophy and cared about it. Over the years, he had become a good friend.

He waited for me to get through the check-out line and walked with me to my car. We took the long way and he asked me about my research. When I finally asked him about Mada, he responded readily. I'd expected him to say she was an "amazing woman," "a great artist," and he did. But he also said, "Mada is a woman who has uprooted personal guilt. She thrives on immersing herself in the world but sets her own destination."

"Where is she going?" I muttered. "Can anyone else go there too?"

He laughed, loosening his grip on his pipe stem for

just a moment. "Do you know where she began?" he asked me.

"The Second World War. In Dresden."

"And what else?"

"She made a new life, from a new and personal place."

"What place?"

"Where . . . common definitions of ethics don't apply."

"Ah yes, ethics," he said. "The modern dilemma. How to be good without outside pressure. What does it mean to stop making value judgements?"

"It means being true to one's own construct," I suggested.

He grunted in disagreement. "Too binding. I think it requires a constant state of awareness, of purpose, yet an inability to state purpose in advance."

"Like the arrow that never reaches the target," I said. "But I think you're describing sainthood."

His pipe waved up and down. "Do you think that describes Mada?"

"No."

"Why not?"

"Not unless we redefine what a saint is."

"Exactly. But we already know she defies definition. Hence some would say she lacks a soul."

"Mada is nothing but soul."

"And yet we know how real her soul is."

"Mada is just an experience," I said, hearing the

sadness in my voice. David immediately sensed its origin.

"And what havoc that plays with your own sense of self, doesn't it?" he asked kindly.

I nodded. Of course he knew her far better, far longer than I. But he wasn't a woman and he wasn't her lover.

"How do we love someone like that?"

We looked away from each other at the trees. He said, "Perhaps the question is not how but why and when?"

"Why is easy. It's impossible not to."

"Ah . . ."

"And when? From the beginning and all the time."

"So why matters after all," he mused.

"Because I can't do otherwise," I stated without emotion. Loving her felt as inevitable as breathing.

We walked companionably for a while, enjoying the mildness of the late summer day on the brink of fall. Already the days were shorter, a first taste of the early nightfalls to come. The sun had begun to set farther south, over the mountains, no longer dropping straight down into the sea. But that afternoon the sun sparkled warmly and the sky was clear and distinctly blue. As we looked seaward from the hill, the calm Pacific promised an eternity of gentle surf. By common agreement we paused at a bench beneath a young redwood.

He spoke first. "Some survivors of the Allied bombings of Europe speak about what happened as terrible but sublime. Can you guess why?"

"Because it was a force they couldn't control," I said.

Mada

"A power greater than anything normal life could contain."

"Vishnu, Kali and the Angel of Death — they explode our ideas of ethics."

"And of beauty."

"Yes."

"The monster deities of the Celts are so formidable; the power of the earth itself, before codes of conduct, before good and evil. The point on which we turn has nothing to do with intellect."

He took his pipe out of his mouth, eyed it and then me with a humorous look.

"Do you know the one about the six people going down on an airplane with only five parachutes?" I shook my head.

"A king, a queen, a president and a vice-president each gave very important reasons why they had to live, having to do with their positions in life. One by one, they grabbed parachutes and jumped. This left the Smartest Man on Earth and a kid, with one chute between them. The Smartest Man on Earth said, "Well, I'm the Smartest Man on Earth, so of course I have to live" and he jumped. The kid sat there for a while, then said. "That was the Smartest Man on Earth and he just took my backpack!"

When I stopped laughing David said, "If only knowing more could always give us the right answers." Then his tone changed.

"At the end of the war, Mada was in Poland with other young Germans. They were working on the farms, trying to feed the hungry German army. She was there

Mada

when the Russian soldiers marched into Poland, killing and raping any German they could find."

I heard my strained voice. "How do you know that?"

"I was a GI posted at an entrance to West Berlin. Mada came across from East Berlin every day to work in the American sector. She practised her English. We talked to each other. I was very lonely too.

"What about Dresden? Was she there?"

"I don't know. But Dresden was the great purifier. Her rich family and all their fascist dreams went up in smoke."

"Fascist?"

He shrugged. "Her brother was a high-ranking officer in the Luftwaffe. The Americans captured him early in the war. He was killed trying to escape."

I took a deep breath. "What happened in Berlin?"

"Mada must have been only fifteen or sixteen, but the communists singled her out because of her family. If she didn't comply, they would kill her." I took a deep breath and David went on, "Then Ricard was there. He'd done very well for himself. He had a big hotel. He began following her, wouldn't leave her alone. One day he bought her papers and she didn't go back to East Berlin." David laughed, "Well, you could hear the glass breaking from there. Rumour had it there was some shuffling around in the Russian hierarchy, even one or two disappearances. It was Ricard. His power was apparently quite extensive and he was determined to protect Mada. Doubtlessly, he saved her life. Eventually, as you know, it would have been much more difficult for Mada, if not impossible, to exit East Berlin."

"Did she want him?"

"It's hard to imagine Mada doing anything against her will. Even then, after everything she had been through, she was her own person. But she was very young. There are ways of persuasion you and I know nothing about. And I am not surprised at Mada's capacity for loyalty and gratitude."

I thought about Ricard taking me to Mada. I wondered what he had wanted her for in Berlin?

As if he heard my thoughts, David said, "Perhaps this will help you. Maybe you can't understand Mada's reasons for doing what she does. Reasons in the usual sense don't apply. But you can trust her feelings for you. Maybe that's all that's left when she's gone," he ended quietly.

He tapped his pipe on the edge of the bench, but there was nothing in it. We sat in silence and then switched to inconsequential topics and parted. I thought I saw new depth in his eyes when he looked at me but couldn't tell why.

Later, I looked over the books I'd brought home. They dealt with a time and place in German history long before her own, but her roots were there. I'd felt the connection from the beginning. Deities had stood on the burning point of becoming human. Or had it been the other way around? Was it humanity's loss of knowledge of its material essence that also prevented it from becoming more than human? Had the rest of us forgotten the alchemy that

Mada

she remembered?

I stood at my window for a long time, looking out as the light faded. The small meadow behind the cabin and the trees and bushes surrounding it held the afterglow that followed the setting of the sun. I remembered the large meadow behind Mada's house up north. We had walked to it on a day when the wildflowers were just beginning to open. Like children in perfect happiness and innocence, we brought each other flowers to see and to smell. We walked, not talking, looking everywhere, enjoying every inch of the land. Across the valleys to the north and to the east lay high ridges fringed with redwoods and fluttering birches, gold, silver and green. The sweet, wild smells of flowers in hidden meadows wafted across to us as we stood at the top of the hill. We went back into the meadow, spread our clothes down and made love on the new blades of grass.

When I looked again at my meadow it had gone to black shapes and shadows. I brought down the blinds and retreated to the study to sit next to the fireplace where I'd lit the second fire of the season. The summer nights had become cold. The rain we'd had earlier in the week and the overcast nights had chilled the countryside rapidly. I stared at my books and my stacks of notes. Then I dressed to go out.

It was Friday night, so I wore my black dress slacks, matching silk shirt and a bolo tie with a black onyx in the clasp. I put on my black boots with silver wingtips. With my black eyes and hair — not so bad, I said to my image

Mada

in the mirror. I went down to the Purple Rose.

The crowd that came in for a drink right after work was just leaving and the serious Friday night crowd was coming in, already buzzed on dinner wine. I bought a Lowenbrau Dark and took it to my corner to watch the DJ set up her equipment. After a few numbers, the place was crowded enough for people to start dancing. I started a second beer and watched couples get high on the beat and on each other.

The darkness, the coloured lights, the classy perfumes and the sharp, sexy clothes brought Mada home to me. In the pit of my gut I felt a fist of desire. I stayed there, bottle dangling from my fingers, lost in my pounding heart. I didn't hear her until the second time she asked me to dance. It was almost painful to give in to the strength of another woman's arms, moving me to the music of a slow Anne Murray. It was the DJ's break and the juke box played. Women who wanted to be close to each other danced slow and tight.

I was pressed against her, feeling her hips moving against mine, her breasts blending with mine. She was easy, made no fast or imposing moves, so when another song followed, the slow downeast sound of Anne's, *"Could I Have This Dance for the Rest of My Life?"* we stayed in each other's arms, moving under the spinning lights. As we danced, I moved my head slightly and our lips came close but didn't touch. Her arms dropped to my waist and brought me closer still and then we were in the centre of the music, barely moving our feet, bodies breathing together, giving in completely to hips and thighs swaying to the beat.

Mada

The next song had a good drum beat. We laughed a little and swung each other around in circles and fancy steps. I put my toes down harder, watching her eyes flash as I raised mine. Then a sad, love-lost Anne Murray sang *". . . but I don't see how time will mend a broken heart, when it's broken all apart . . ."* and we drifted to the table for some cold beer.

She leaned back, watching the other dancers, knowing I was looking at her, taking in her feathered blonde hair and the gold softness of her skin where her collarbones blended into the curve of her breasts. And then the slow, soft music played again, *"I'll always remember that magical moment when I held you close to me, as we moved together, I knew forever, you're all I need . . ."* Without a word she moved to the dance floor. We whirled apart, then came towards each other slowly, watching the other's eyes until our breasts touched. Her eyes closed first.

Now we barely touched, turned on just by brushing against each other, feeling the electricity of flesh against cloth. Pleasure built between us like another body we shared. In the middle of a step she took my hand and led me back to an empty hallway between the dance floor and private offices. The music throbbed through the wall and she put me against it and gently leaned her body towards me. I let my breath out and put my fingers on her hips, pulling her to me. She kissed me then, parting my lips with nudges of her mouth until our tongues met. And then I slipped from under her. Hearing my boot heels tapping on

Mada

the hard floor of the corridor, I kept walking until I was outside, fumbling for my keys, afraid to turn around. I drove straight from the Purple Rose even though I was going in the wrong direction, afraid that if I saw her, I wouldn't be able to keep driving away. Not knowing where I was going, I was afraid of staying, afraid of making love, afraid I might feel with someone else the passion I had only felt with Mada, afraid that would ruin it.

I drove around the curves to my cabin, crazy with guilt for almost betraying what I felt for Mada and for that lovely woman I had left without explanation in the hallway. I fell into my bed without turning on a light in the house. My boots on, my clothes wet from body heat and sex, I held my head in my arms, still feeling the walls throbbing and the sweet demands of her mouth.

I felt the heat of her body, but her face was Midge's. I saw Midge's clear soft skin, so white against the deep black of my hair and I saw Midge's gentle blue eyes that could turn from ice to deep-sea blue as she saw my pleasure at her blondness, at her slim stature, at my wanting her as much as she wanted me. She came away from the dance floor, led me into a hallway covered with photographs — the two of us doing everything two naked women could do with their bodies and their mouths and their hands. Midge and me.

"Would you be my partner every night, when we're together, it feels right, would you be my partner for the rest of my life. . ." Is that what I promised Midge? Blonde, blue-eyed, trusting Midge. Making the same promises to

Mada

myself, knowing there would always be Mada? Had I wanted for once to remove Mada from the space between us, to make way for Midge and I finally to lean towards each other, to feel the wall throbbing and let our bodies yield to an orgasm that had waited so long to happen, a climax that would hurt and then take our pain away forever?

CHAPTER 5

I STUDIED. TWO OF THE GRANTS I'D APPLIED FOR CAME through: a small one to travel to New York, then to Washington D.C., to study materials in the Library of Congress; the other, more substantial, would support my research for a year. I was thankful for the freedom of movement they gave me and took time to organise my activities, planning to go east sometime during the winter.

I went on with my life, but all the time I waited for her, for her voice on the telephone, for a message on my answering machine or a note in my box on campus, for anything that would tell me I could reach that ecstasy again. Nothing else was real. It wasn't how I wanted it, and there were moments that I forgot her as I ran on the beach, breathing hard against the wind, bruising my feet, falling on the sand. But the time would always come when I'd sit quietly looking out at the Pacific, drawing outlines of her body and her face in the air.

Mada

If I'd thought the rest of my life would be like that, it would have been unbearable, but I thought only of the next time. Her version of our love was all I had and it was forever slipping away into a time I hadn't yet lived. The only moments I really had were woven from the impulse threads of unborn stars. I waited, and I hated it. I threw her away a thousand times on slips of paper, saying goodbye but knowing I didn't mean it.

One day, trying to undo that mood, I drove up the north coast highway. The morning had been sweatshirt cold, but the fog burned off by midday. The soft afternoon sunshine hinted of the long days of Indian Summer soon to come. Fields of green onions and broccoli, ripe with butterflies and bees, stretched green carpets to the far edge of high cliffs, then fell away into blue water.

I'd been driving slowly and peacefully and had decided to stop at a restaurant that had a reputation for healthy, top-quality food. As I was looking for a parking place, I saw the Riley suitably wedged between a new Beamer and a Jaguar.

I went in and got a table near the window where I could look across the highway at the sea. In full view of the bar in the next room, I ate clam chowder and the thick dark bread that came with it and wiped my mouth on a white cloth napkin. It was Ricard, of course, and an elegant woman in a green suit.

As I was deciding on coffee, he was at the waiter's elbow, saying "You'll take your coffee in the bar, won't you?"

Mada

The waiter followed me. Ricard and the woman sat on bar stools. Ricard motioned me between them. The woman's beautiful legs were sheathed in silk. Her name was Marsha, she lived in Malaga and her lips were sensuous and hard at the same time. She looked me over as if I were a Kowloon girl with a number on my chest.

"Rough, but lovely, as you said, Ricard. Won't you have a dollop of something with that coffee, my dear?"

"Why not?" I said and ordered a liqueur.

It arrived in a thin glass with gold trim and a red lip. It was a deep apricot colour, like the skin of some Latin women in the sun.

They watched me swallow. The drink burned going down. Marsha saw this and smiled, showing perfect porcelain teeth. I took my eyes away first, looking around the bar for some casual normality in this seemingly harmless meeting.

No one mentioned Mada, but she was there as we talked, inventing amusements to tell and turning our secret thoughts over with toothpicks — theirs from previous sour gimlets and embalmed olives.

I didn't touch the coffee but perversely accepted another drink from Marsha and switched to Pernod to have something to look at. I stared at the swirling white liquid, as she all but raised happy eyebrows. Ricard smiled smugly and they traded innuendos over my head. Soon after, Marsha offered that we'd be much more comfortable in her "darling summer cottage" just around a redwood or two.

Mada

I stood up to leave, but Ricard stopped me with a stiff arm across my path and a decidedly nasty grin on his face. I realised he was drunk — they both were. He told Marsha to try harder. To her credit, she shrugged, unhooked her eyes and showing me some hefty cleavage for the last time, turned back to the bar. The smile soured on Ricard's face, but we said our goodbyes and I left.

Blinking a little in the sunlight, I cheerfully kicked stones on the way to my car. I tossed the keys up and down, put them back in my pocket and crossed the road, over the railroad tracks, picking my way like a happy fool down the steep trail to the beach.

I ran without my shoes, a little crookedly, in the direction of the water, shocking myself with an incoming wave that soaked me to the knees and sprayed my face with cold, salty water. I suddenly wanted to immerse myself in it. Back and forth against the waves I ran, feet splashing, arms swinging until I couldn't take another step. Then I flung myself down on a dune. My head fell against the sand.

Arms out, I breathed in big deep gulps of sea air, madly, gratefully happy for having Mada to love. We were this earth, this rock cliff, this sandy beach, locked together in an embrace as old as earth-spirits and as new as our discovery of each other's bodies. Our love was now, and this was all the time I'd ever have of loving her. Then I heard Ricard.

"What makes you think you can be something to her?" He spoke thickly. "Do you know how many there have been?" He blocked the sun with his shadow as I, gritty with sand, turned to face him.

"It doesn't matter. No one else matters to me, just me and her. Not even you," I lied.

"You're a number," he went on. "Worth, perhaps, a word . . . "

"If it's like that," I cut in, "why are you so worried about it?"

Watching him blink, mouth askew, I almost regretted saying it.

"Mada likes lovely faces and fresh bodies like yours."

Then I really didn't understand him. "Why are you talking about her like that?"

He waved his arms, sinking his feet further into the sand. "I made her. I can talk about her any way I please."

"What do you mean?"

"I saw what a beautiful lover of women she would be — and I made her that way," he spit out. "I made her."

I knew I could shout something, but it wouldn't make any difference. He slung the words after me as I struggled away.

"I made her! I can take her apart again . . ." At last his voice faded behind the waves and the sand dunes.

An insane, drunken man, I told myself. They all drop their facades at one time or another and he'll regret it more than most. I was angry and shaking with disgust, remembering that first night and how smooth, impersonal — even kind — he'd been. Today he had followed me down to the beach, scuffing the leather on his expensive shoes, staining his tailored clothes with sweat, ranting about my relationship with Mada.

It had never been a one night-stand for me, it was impossible to define or even describe. Maybe I'd never be comfortable with it, but she wanted me too, followed me like I'd followed her. I knew — the two of us on that same small-town college stage so long ago, the trail of her reading engagements from New York to Arizona, my own compulsive slingshot movements from coast to coast, those anguished months in San Francisco, then here in her haven in the redwoods — we had to come face to face again, had to give ourselves to a passion that had redrawn geography and other people's lives to exist.

Perhaps we should all be afraid of it, I thought, scrambling for a foothold on the high ground at the top of the steep climb. I got in my car without looking for Marsha and pointed myself north towards my original destination. But the time for going there had passed. A few miles later, there was an opportunity to turn around. I took it and went back.

Getting into town, I stopped at the Pizza Pub, leaned against the car to watch the sunlight on the rooftops of Westlands, and feel the presence of other, saner people nearby. Why hadn't I told Mada everything from the beginning? I hadn't known it all. Did she? Did anyone?

Pizza, gut-sucking, sloppy, sopping, raunchy pizza and beer. "Rough," she'd said, Miss Green Suit. But she'd wanted me on sight. How easy it was for some to recognise anything and anyone who could serve their tiny selves and block out what didn't.

"Hey, Raquel!" Mo waved me over to their table and I let up on my sticky bubble-gum, self-involvement to wave at a few friends, music students throwing their egos around in a laughing way.

"Hey, Mo," I answered him, the brilliant piano player of funky blues playing spoons on beer mugs.

"Be a one-two," Harvey Driscoll said, between snorts on a paper kazoo. I obliged with an entrance riff on an over-turned pizza plate. Coco said, "Raquel, you're wasted on those dusty books." His greasy hair hung in front of his ears, his tongue was clenched between his crooked teeth and he was playing the sweetest skins you'd ever want to hear with a fanned-out roll of newspaper.

"Juice, give me some juice!" yelled Mo, and I did, including the backs of two chairs in my rack of instruments. We played a pretty good rendition of Brubeck's *Summertime Blues*. Arien waited until we came up, laughing, for air, then said at my shoulder, "Raquel, you doing anything later?" Sweet words, sweet woman.

"When later?"

"Well, like after this," Arien caught me up.

"Better get her while you can." Driscoll told her, "before she buries herself in paper again."

"Look, Arien," I started. She was looking at me intently, open and expectant. "Okay, sure."

"Do some living. Ah, loving," said Coco. We laughed, but his brown eyes stayed serious. Maybe I was being obvious. They were friends, they liked me. Maybe if

I was half as easy, I could be like them: trusting and involved.

"Raquel, you're the original innocent," said Coco, taking a wild swing at making his hair go back. "Don't take it to your grave."

"If you only knew," I said.

"Get lost, birdies," said Mo and pushed us out the door. I followed Arien's throaty MG down to the entrance to Route 1, then across town by the old Hidalgo bridge and into the snug, shoe-box neighbourhoods of Dolphin Flats.

A portion of the marina intersected at Beach Avenue and we followed it west to the pier where Arien had docked her boat. A twenty-six foot sail boat with backup engines, she lived on it, but seldom took it into the open sea.

I admired her life in that small a space and had looked for something similar before moving into my cabin, but the waiting list for slips was just too long. I took a change of clothes I had in the car with me and dressed before coming out on deck, barefoot, to watch the sunset. We drank Anchor Steam, feet up on the rail, rocking in the surge that came in from the levy. Seagulls circled, dropping down for tidbits before settling for the night. Overturned catamarans drying on the beach fired briefly in the last rays of the dying sun. The light softened, then retreated until we were in darkness. Then we heard the distant barking of sea lions above the gentle splashing of waves against the hull.

Arien clearly had something to say.

"Arien, I'm here where you wanted me and I'm listening." I could feel her looking back at me, though I could barely see the shine in her eyes and on her lips. She was stiff, tense.

"My life is tied up in doing the right things," she said. Her voice was low, almost a whisper, "There's no room for feelings."

"Without rules, society would fall apart." I leaned towards her. "Who knows what people might do, even what friends would do? It could be disastrous."

She shook her head. "It's what we don't do, can't do and want to do, have to do, that makes us — me — crazy." She talked with her hands, making quick, eloquent gestures, as though she would break without them.

"What do you want to do, Arien?"

She swung up on the railing without answering and looked down at me.

"Am I stopping you now?"

"Yes," she said. "I mean me too. "We're women who love women and it's so hard to be open, to talk to each other, to ask for something that means getting physically close."

Her voice was ready to break. "This isn't theory, this is real! Every move we make towards each other is so singularly interpreted. It makes us so limited in our expression, so isolated. And we're trying to be better, do it better than men?"

Mada

"Arien." I made her go below deck, faced her and gathered her into my arms.

"I don't know why you hurt. I'm not sure what you need. But if this is what you want, you can have it from me."

She nodded yes, my lips against her hair.

We lay down on the bed. I caressed her face, kissing her head, feeling her thighs press against my legs. Warm, smelling slightly of flowers, she simply wanted to feel another woman's body close. I wanted that too. I needed it too. I wanted to be touched, without thinking or caring about sex, wanted her to touch the place I loved from, to touch my loneliness and my confusion.

As the water rocked us together in that small compact space, the bed was just big enough. We took turns cradling each other, our breasts soft lovely mysteries without words. When I felt her start to sleep, mouth wet on my shoulder, I slowly got up. Moving carefully on deck, I took my gear and left the boat. The night was unusually clear and cold, the stars loose in the sky and close to earth. It was wonderful to be eased of pain and loneliness, to feel strengthened and firm in my body, a lesbian woman real to another and to myself.

When I got home close to midnight, Mada's message was waiting for me. I called her and went to her the next day.

CHAPTER 6

MADA OPENED THE DOOR, BECKONED ME IN, WAITED for me to turn around and close the door, waited for me to turn back and kiss her.

I smelled her restlessness as soon as she let me in. It had an edge of sadness. She moved back to stand by the wall. Her ankle-length caftan had the first few buttons open at the throat and at the hem above her bare feet. She never took her eyes off me; their green spun into the deeper green of her dress as I watched her face tell me what to do. She breathed through her mouth, in quick short pants, pulling me to her, then stopping me an arm's length away.

I reached out to touch her with my fingertips. We started, broke contact, then came together again. She let me explore her body, taut under the caftan's soft folds, filled with desire but making me come closer a fraction of an inch at a time, then letting me open her legs and take her with my mouth at last. Tasting her soft flood of pleasure from my knees, I served her as I would a goddess. Afterwards, holding me, she came all the way into my arms and we lay together, her breath now deep and warm on my neck.

"They were women without love," she murmured.

I lay perfectly still.

"He knew he couldn't have me. Even then. He wanted payment for keeping me in the West — to watch how I loved."

I saw that delicate and beautiful woman-child David had told me about.

"He found women for me. They were always the wives of powerful men."

She turned away and lay on her back, eyes closed. "The first wasn't much older than I, the wife of an army officer, a grey man with polished boots and a bald head. He disgusted me the most, but she was so afraid of what I could give her and so afraid of revealing herself in front of him."

I sat up. Her pulse beat just above her breast, and though her eyes were open, she didn't see me.

"We were on a large bed in a very large room, lit up as a show for impotent men of distinction who sat in the dark. I took her face, like this, so she could see only me. They were nothing. Nothing! I held her face so we saw only each other. While I made love to her, I made her forget them. There was no other way, miene liebe. No other way for me."

She stood and moved to the window, her hair black against the white draperies, her eyes dark with memories.

"From the beginning, he made records: films, photographs, lists of names. Later, he put in television monitors. He had control of my legal affairs, my finances. At first I knew nothing and then he had his hands on everything."

"Mada, that night . . . ?"

"Nothing. He gets nothing from that room — it's my sanctuary."

She smiled wryly, "He grants me that small peace. Before it didn't matter. But with Madeleine and with you, he gets nothing."

"That explains his mood these days," I said, in a voice that sounded like we were talking about the weather.

"He told me how he met you. He said you were easy to convince, easy to arouse."

"Bastard!"

She came to me, touched me. "Never mind, miene liebe. I know he lies. He can't punish me that way."

She ordered from room service but scarcely ate. We sat outside on the balcony, high above the beach as trucks and cars streamed by on the wharf below. In the distance the ferris wheel on the boardwalk turned in the sky. She sent me away but asked me to come back that night. I closed the drapes, set the thermostat for her and left.

At nightfall I drove to the beach near my cabin and tried to run the tightness from my muscles. As I ran, my

Mada

body felt powerful and I wanted her with a fury. Mada opened the door to me, ready to leave. She had already reserved a cottage near 17 Mile Drive in Monterrey. I drove the Mercedes, stopped at a fish place she liked in Carmel. Except for the pensione on Powell Street, we'd never made love twice in the same bed. Now I knew why.

She was playful over dinner, talking to the waiter and the bus boy, charming everyone who saw her. I fell more in love with her every moment.

The place we went to was modest and private. A small garden separated each cottage, and past a grove of Monterrey pines, the waves crashed against a sea wall, their fury muted by the trees. The closeness of Big Sur brought back that night at Nepenthe. I asked her what had happened.

"That night — what do you know about it?" She took my hand in hers.

"Now I think Midge feared she'd lose you forever if you and I were together, even once.

"Maybe."

"She had me, but she was in love with you, my darling."

"And you, Mada?"

She steadied me with her eyes. "You know, Raquel, for me love is always simple. I wanted both of you. It was never hard."

She squeezed my hand. "Midge brought you to me. She arranged everything, but that night — "

"I drove up from San Francisco," I interrupted.

"I raced a sports car over Bixby Creek in the dark."

I laughed. "I felt so damn immortal because I was going to be with you. After all that time. I wasn't afraid of anything. No matter what happened, I thought it couldn't be wrong."

"Yes."

"But Midge was in the parking lot waiting for me when I got there. Everything had been fine and now she was angry. She said we didn't need her. She said the play was over. What did she mean?"

"She didn't explain herself to me. Just said she'd show us our plan wouldn't work. I didn't understand. I said it was what we had planned together, her and I. It was what she wanted. She said that you wouldn't come, that you belonged to her alone. She cried."

"And I asked her what had happened. She said everything was distorted, mean. She said it was only fair because she was the one who had made it happen. I tried to talk to her, but she wouldn't listen. It was what she wanted. She made us want it too and then fucked us over." I felt angry and bitter, but it had nothing to do with Midge.

"Tell me, Raquel. Tell me now."

"Maybe what she said was true." I felt the blood drain from my face with fear.

"Maybe I did it all. I got her interested in me, got her to come back from her mother's house where she was safe, pushed her work in the direction I wanted."

"You inspired her. No one else could."

Mada

"But I looked away from the drugs. At first I even joined her. I used her illusions, exploited her fantasies. Did you know about those photographs? I mean before the retrospective?"

"I'm not sure."

"Mada."

"That night — maybe that's what she had in her hand. She had a large manila envelope. The proof sheets, maybe?"

I remembered. "Oh God! She kept waving this envelope in my face, shouting, `You think you know everything — this is what we could have had. But you lied to me.' I didn't know what she was talking about and she wouldn't tell me."

"She told me something before . . ."

"Mada, you saw her earlier?"

"Before I left San Francisco. She put the camera on a timer and got into bed beside me. She told me she had something to give me later, something wonderful."

We were silent for a few minutes. Why had Midge come to Nepenthe without showing us the pictures? Why had she broken the three of us apart?

Brooding, I said, "I went sneaking up the path in the dark anyway, just to catch a glimpse of you. I saw you up on the terrace, standing near a table with a glass in your hand, smiling . . ."

Suddenly, that night's raw grief, a weight I'd carried with me from San Francisco, broke like a flood.

"We did it, Mada. You and me. We killed her."

She said very quietly, "My darling, if you really believe that, then you must leave me now." If only she had known how exact her words would be. If only she hadn't spoken them.

"We're fucked people, Mada. We're fucked all the way. Jake was right — we let her play with a loaded gun until she blew her brains out."

"No. You can't believe that. She alone knew what happened to her that night."

Then I said the cruellest words I could have spoken: "We fucked over her dead body, Mada!"

She stopped me from saying more, made me look at her. "You and I weren't together that night, Raquel. And you were never, never her lover."

But I couldn't listen. "I suggested all of it to her. I turned her on, then kept her hanging. It was finally set that you and I would, would. . . and it pushed her over the edge."

The demon in my heart rose up and swallowed me. "We stopped at the knife's edge," I cried. "But then she took it in the gut."

Mada said quietly, firmly. "Then why? Why did she make the pictures of the three of us together?"

"I don't know."

"Think about it, Raquel. She made them because she believed it was the only way for us. She wanted to say something to you after everything was gone. It was all she could say — to me and to you! It was her gift to us."

Then I cried as though my soul were leaking away. I

didn't know how much it cost Mada to hold me, to feel me change under her hands, feel me leave her. I asked her to drop me at the all-night Greyhound station in Monterrey and I went inside without watching her drive away.

On the trip back I sat staring into the darkness like a mad woman. When I got off the bus I didn't look for a cab. I walked for two hours from the centre of town to my cabin on Grange Road. I stayed in the cabin, except to go out for food, most of which I left in the bags it came in. She called, but I ignored her messages. After a few days, the calls stopped.

One night I went into my study, threw a few books into an empty suitcase, without looking at them, and jammed in all the clean underwear I had left. I showered for the first time in days and washed my hair, then packed a few final clothes. I ate what was still good in the fridge, then drove to the San Jose airport, left my car in the long-term parking area and caught the red-eye to LA. A few hours later I caught an early morning flight to New York.

CHAPTER 7

F ALL IN THE BIG APPLE. THE TOURISTS HAD LEFT WASH- ington Square, returning it to old men, homeless Blacks and light-hearted students from NYU and Cooper Union. The skies turned murky grey and the leaves grew sparse, leaving the trees gaunt. Cold winds began to blow down the street canyons of Manhattan. Hawkers in the East Village put on the determined faces they'd wear until spring.

I rented a room above Tompkins Square, at the edge of an area where the buildings were even seedier, with toilets that doubled as chairs or hiding places for drugs in apartments where plumbing never worked. Inside museums and art galleries, I looked at the faces of people who were looking at the artifacts. There was no one I recognised, no one to be recognised by. One time I went out of my way to go to a private screening of an old foreign film, but I left when the self-conscious, affected analysis started. I rode on subway trains to the end of the line and rode them back again, watching the red, yellow, blue and green lights flash as we hurtled down tunnels. As the interior lights flashed on and off, other riders looked like ill-dressed manikins, hoping to arrive at a better destination.

When I had nowhere to go I walked across the Brooklyn Bridge, reciting passages of Hart Crane aloud. I strode up and down Tom Tryon Park or took the Staten Island Ferry, leaning over the side to watch the dirty, churning waters flowing below. Day or night, it made no difference. I went wherever my restlessness drove me. The world could have been painted black and I wouldn't have noticed. I was invisible, a shadow, drawn to the light of other people's lives to see from the outside what ordinary happiness was like.

At first I tried to study, but my books stayed shut and note cards blank as I stared at the walls in library research rooms, like a would-be painter playing with light and shade. I was interested in nothing, felt nothing. Once in a while, the sight of a beautiful woman's hair, a particular book in a shop window, or the smell of black bread from the Russian bakery on Second Avenue, where stout-armed caring women from the Ukraine greeted me, stirred me. I followed people then: a short-haired woman walking her dog, going home to a well-lit, secure building on East 10th Street, a young mother at the Brooklyn Zoo, showing her toddler the Bengal tiger. Sometimes I thought I could speak, make one small contact, but the moment always died like a failed spark. When I probed myself for familiar feelings I paid the price at night with guilt-ridden, dismembered dreams of Midge's death.

Was she still alive the morning I pulled into a motel outside Los Angeles? Was she still alive as I fell into the empty bed and slept, exhausted and without remorse, convinced I had acted for the best? Was her death unplanned and unhurried? Or did she cry as she heated up the spoon, not bothering with cotton, tied herself off quickly, to destroy desire, because it promised her life, and came to nothing? Did she think I'd walk in and take the Death Angel from her hand one more time? When she saw the syringe fill with her blood did she forget how bad she felt? Red, red beauty backing up in a swollen vein — a kick better than any engorged fantasy of cunt — endless, nodding pleasure.

I wasn't there when they carried you out, my lovely treasure, the sheeted stretcher, the flashing red lights, the paramedics too late. They took you through the very door I'd walked through a hundred times, then turned back to you and kissed you.

After one of those nights I would walk myself to exhaustion, trying to forget Mada. But she lived on beneath my skin, sealed in a bloodless envelope of memory. In time, a pattern formed in my wanderings: up the Avenue of the Americas, along the fringe of Central Park to 103rd Street, then a few minutes rest on one of the benches facing the street. The days shortened and the first snow fell and quickly melted into ankle-deep slush at the curbs. Then it was colder and more snow came and stayed, painting the small hills and meadows of Central Park white. Finally, the chestnut vendors came out, their wagons of roasting chestnuts making small islands of warmth along the long frozen sidewalks uptown. Like others, I huddled against the cold as I went to my bench to catch the few rays of sun that passed over us.

I began to carry a sketch book, bought for its blank pages when I was still trying to think up ideas for my research. I began to draw little things: a tree, an empty bench, then the contours of my small corner of the park and buildings across the way. Finally, I sketched lone walkers and groups of two or three as they walked by or rested on park benches. The skill and perception that had come easily to me as a young student, before I had given them up for academic pursuits, swiftly returned to hand and eye. While I drew, I began to look at things again, to delight in their visual essence, to come to conclusions based only on an object's position in space, and later, on the relation between light and colour. I began to exchange a few words now and then with my bench companions.

One day, as I looked up from sketching the young child standing beside me, my eyes still fresh with her innocence, I saw Mada. She had emerged from a cab at the corner of 103rd and was crossing the street towards my row of benches. Heart pounding, I had gotten up to leave when she saw me. I'd already turned away, but her voice stopped me. In calling my name she pulled apart the stitching in my crudely mended heart. Painful love spilled out, undeniable and urgent. I saw it too in her face and body, in the flaring green of her eyes.

She didn't try to touch me but said, "Come with me."

"No . . . I can't." I pleaded. Her lips trembled, but she nodded and motioned me to walk beside her along the path to the park zoo.

I walked stiffly, trying to rein in my spirit, but it was too late for me to go on without her. Our passion lived and I would never have the strength or the will to leave it again. I had lost her once, but no matter what happened next, now we were together.

"You're thin, my darling," she said as we leaned against the leopard cage just before feeding time.

I returned her look. "Mada."

And she knew. The leopard came down from her perch in a high tree, growled once and looked around with fierce, hungry eyes. Then she gave herself to eating, tearing away chunks of raw meat, while holding the bulk of it with huge padded paws. We walked back to the small restaurant at the zoo entrance to get something to eat. Only now, after we had acknowledged our love, could we think of anything so mortal as thirst or hunger. Ready to leave, she held back from asking how to reach me, wrote down a number on a matchbook and put it in my coat pocket. I tore a page from my sketch book, put my address on it and gave it to her. Our hands never touched. She walked back the way we'd come.

After I sat for several minutes, I took a different path

Mada

west until I came out on the street and found a BMT stop. I rode the subway to Bleeker Street and walked the rest of the way home. The milk and orange juice were ice-cold in the grocery box outside on the window sill. I drank both, then fell asleep in the armchair by the window, cradling the empty cartons in my lap.

The sound of the clanging radiator, the heat coming on, woke me at dawn. It was colder, snowing again, large white feathers falling straight down. I opened the window and stuck my head out. As far as I could see lay a blanket of new snow, softly white over the still, bleak streets. I wanted to shout out my love, pour into the snow's pristine promise a new beginning. Mada. Mada, can you hear me? In that second between birth and first breath, her answer came; Raquel. I closed the window, put on my coat and boots and ran swiftly down the stairs to the street. I took the IRT to Grand Central, changed lines, got an uptown train, getting off at the last stop, and went straight to a phone. It rang twice before she answered, awake.

"Can you come out?"

"Yes."

"Take the A train to the end of the line. I'll be waiting for you."

"Three-quarters of an hour," she said.

"Mada . . . "

"Yes?"

"Nothing."

"Soon, my darling."

I walked back and forth along the tracks, in the

Mada

steam mixing with the cold air of the subway and the smell of dirt, urine and oil. A few poor working souls, cold fingers clenching bag lunches, stood across the tracks, waiting for the downtown train. It came and left; I was alone again. I leaned over the track, looked back into the darkness — red lights, blue lights glowing in the distance. I walked to the end of the platform, reading the graffiti on the pillars and torn transit posters. I climbed a weigh scale and saw my face in the mirror. My eyes were large and black. With a shock, I saw my face, still gaunt and flushed, like someone recovering from a terrible illness. The pea coat swallowed me up. I pushed back my hair with my fingers; it was thick and alive; I looked down the tracks again. A pinpoint of red in the far tunnel blinked off; green flashed on.

I saw her move to the front of the train as it barrelled into the station, swaying and slamming to a stop. I ran alongside the car, anxious for the doors to open. She came out at last. We went up the stairs together, coming into the sudden glare of the snow-covered ground. To our right, high on the hill among the trees, stood the Cloisters. We stood face to face, our breath coming out in little puffs of white. As we stood under a streetlamp the light went out. It was no longer snowing. We were alone, surrounded by gleaming snow. She linked her arm with mine and we walked towards the river. The only sounds were our breathing and our feet crunching on new snow.

We saw the wide, rolling Hudson streaming by below and looked across at the distant greys and browns

Mada

of the wooded New Jersey shore. While we watched, the lights went out on the George Washington bridge, leaving only the lights in her eyes, bright green like new leaves in spring. I wanted to kiss her then. She saw it in my eyes and smiled. I raised her collar to the wind that gusted now and then; she took my hand and put it with hers into the ample pocket of her overcoat. We walked down and around, then up the trail to the Cloisters. It felt right not to talk. The soft voices of medieval music drew us to the Cloisters' glassed-in courtyard and we settled there against a pillar in a corner.

She kept my hand in her pocket, her fingers warming mine. Wanting only to bask in the warmth of her love, I closed my eyes. Much later I felt her stir, her lips close to my ear, "Look, miene liebe. Open your eyes." A few people, dark bulks on the floor and against the walls, were observing the silence. Everyone looked towards the courtyard where the first flakes of new snow had just begun to fall on the bare branches of the rose bushes. Suspended in time, I felt her lips on my cheek.

"Here, filled with hundreds of years of contemplation, where so many have known perfect love, promise me, Raquel, that you won't leave me again. I couldn't stand it." There in the shadows of medieval France, the snow falling silently a few feet away, I promised. She moved her lips to mine and we kissed, our lips barely touching. The Gregorian chants in the background awakened in me an impulse to speak Spanish, the language of my mother: *Hay, Mada, como te quiero. Te quiero para*

Mada

siempre. Mada answered in German: *Ich liebe dich, Raquel.*

Together we listened peacefully to the music until many people filled the space. Cruelty and deception did not exist. Protected by time and our sister-spirits in the stone, we were free. We went outside where a few wisps of snow still fell and the grey clouds had changed to white and bright light blushed on the horizon. On the train we stood beside one another, letting its swaying push us together and pull us apart again. As I left Grand Central, she didn't wave, but her eyes never left mine as long as I was in sight. It had not come easy for either of us, but our vow of love echoed over and over again in my heart. The memory of that one chaste kiss would be all I needed to carry her inside me for a long, long time.

When I got home I took another look at what she had written her telephone number on: a ticket to her benefit performance at Theatre Mnasidika, off-Broadway, the following Sunday. It would be the next to last weekend before Christmas.

CHAPTER 8

I KNEW SOMETHING WAS WRONG THE MOMENT I HEARD THE heavy-handed knock on my door. There were two of them. They looked me and the room over. With their short hair, starched collars and identical trench coats they were inverse copies of each other, one tall and blond, the other tall and dark. They waved ID's that were identical, except for the pictures and names. "Agent Clarence White," said the blond one in a soft, southern drawl.

"Mr Black, I presume?" I said to the other, but he didn't get the joke. He looked me up and down with a sneer calculated to make me feel naked.

"You are acquainted with Mada von Brecht?" asked White.

"I think you know I am."

"Maybe she should be on the list too," said the dark

one. Rush he said his name was. He came and stood very close to me.

"Well," said White, "she's being investigated." Rush was watching for my reaction.

"What do you mean?"

"We're going to bring her up on charges," said White, unbuttoning his trench coat one button at a time. I had the absurd feeling that at any moment he was going to expose himself to me. His fingers stopped on the last button.

"Charges, including prostitution and contributing to the delinquency of minors."

"You're crazy," I said. Rush drew his breath in and White narrowed his pale, transparent eyes. He had a nervous tic in one cheek and his collar seemed to be cutting off his breath. The soft tone was all act, as he very clearly said, "Dyke trash. Kraut immigrant garbage." Rush sneered back at him. I heard the wetness as he pulled his lips away from his teeth and smacked them at his partner.

"I was born here," I said unnecessarily.

Agent Rush screwed up his face like he was going to cry. "When are you people going to learn to be good Americans?" he said. "Just look at this place." I looked around. It looked like you'd expect a place across from Tompkins Square to look. Not all that bad; there was heat and a bed that stood above the floor on legs. But that wasn't what he was looking at. It was the table covered with drawing books, pencils, newsprint and art postcards from the Guggenheim and the Smithsonian. I backed up to

Mada

the window, guilty, at the very least, of not working nine to five.

"Why are you here? What do you want?"

"This is a friendly warning, sister. Because you're a woman and an American," said White, all drawl again. "Stay away from the von Brecht woman."

Meanwhile, Agent Rush was rifling the pages of my large sketch book. "Any dirty pictures in here?"

Agent White motioned with his head and Rush stopped, but his big round thumb remained pressing the cover. He saw my eyes go from his hand to his face, and something must have showed in my look because rage twisted his mouth. "I wouldn't waste my seed on you!" he shouted, sounding like someone he'd seen in a movie and worked at remembering — the stance and the words. But his anger was very real; he wanted to break my neck for who I was. I tried to walk towards the door, but White blocked my way. I curbed my fear and walked around him before he could move.

"You haven't given me a reason."

"Har, har. She wants a reason," White said, following me. His teeth were grinding so hard his jaw could crack. Rush made a throw-away gesture with his hand.

"Let's just take her out with the rest of the shit," he said. He was through with my notebooks now and sidestepped to the door. It was getting very crowded here.

"Maybe in a plastic bag," said White. Rush must have owned only one good line because he used it again, finishing with, "Fucking lezzie!" White took his arm,

Mada

opened the door, steered him through it, consumed and muttering.

Agent White was all crisp business now. "Remember what we said — stay away from the von Brecht woman."

I closed the door after them, locked it and watched from the window as they walked across the street and around the corner. Fighting nausea, I stuffed my feet into boots, dashed down the stairs and across the street. I poked my head around the corner just in time to see White and Rush get into a colourless, late-model Mercedes parked in a red zone. Strange car for German-haters, I thought. Rush drove, cutting off a Ford as he pushed himself into traffic. I glimpsed a badly dented rear bumper before the traffic closed around them. I stayed pressed to the corner building for a few minutes, then hurried to the basement liquor store at the end of my block. I dialled Mada's number, let it ring several times, then hung up and tried again. No answer. When I went back outside I was freezing.

Back in my room, I opened the window to air out their awful presence. Then I wrapped up and took the subway to 103rd. I walked back and forth, waiting for Mada, but after a couple of hours, I couldn't take the cold anymore. I didn't know where she was or how to find her. I cursed myself for not finding out more when I had the chance. Her phone kept ringing, but no one picked it up. For the next few days I felt watched no matter where I went. I haunted the area around 103rd, standing in doorways, making countless useless calls. I wanted to move to

Mada

another room, but didn't dare in case she tried to reach me. More than once I saw the Mercedes with the crushed rear chrome parked within three blocks of my building, but I didn't see the two men again.

On Thursday I came back from another fruitless vigil uptown, to find a telegram tacked on my door. Fortunately, the boy was just leaving; perhaps my mail was being monitored as well. The envelope shook in my hands. There were only three words: Gregorian — same — day.

On Friday night I set my alarm for three in the morning — if White and Rush slept, I figured they did it then. I left a light burning, packed a lunch, and assuming I was being followed anyway, took the train to Harlem. I switched directions twice, hopped on another downtown train and got off at Bowling Green. I ran across the street to the other side, caught the first train leaving the station and got on an uptown train at Grand Central. If the men were still looking for me there, I would have seen them. But no, it was just me and a couple of winos — out cold on the cement floor. Other times the train could have rocked me to sleep, but I was too keyed up for that now.

I climbed out of the subway at 87th, my ears ringing from all the riding, and after ten minutes, caught a taxi to go the rest of the way. The cabbie was too New York to ask me what I was doing out there before dawn, with a blizzard in the forecast. He just took my fare and sped away in a blast of exhaust. I trudged up the path to the main door of the Cloisters and huddled down in the corner at the top to wait. There was a vent near the sidewalk and a few gusts of warm air came out at intervals.

I didn't think, couldn't imagine anything. I remembered my mother telling me *Los inocentes no viven en este mundo.* Innocence doesn't last long in this world. Get strong. Our vows of love the week before had been made as though our pasts did not exist, as though Ricard and his team of dirty men — (I had no doubt his hand was in this) — did not exist. He'd sent them to intimidate and degrade. I didn't know what they'd done to Mada and it was just the beginning. It doesn't matter, I thought. I won't let anything keep us apart. But I wasn't sure. How much was this love worth to Mada? Enough to risk her reputation? Her life? And what about my life? I wavered between feeling like Superwoman and feeling mindlessly terrified, but I knew which one I had to be when I saw her face.

I was stunned at the suffering in her eyes, grey-green with trouble, her cheekbones sharp in her face, and afraid of how cold her hands felt when she gave them to me.

"They came to you?" she asked. I nodded.

"Then you know?"

"I want to hear it from you," I said.

"After we saw each other in Monterrey, that's when it began."

"They were out there?"

"No, no. Letters, messages left for me at my hotel desk, at the bar of a restaurant. Three times I went out and they followed me."

I remembered her phone messages to me. "Mada,

I'm sorry." Then it struck me, "You didn't think that I . . .?"

She shook her head and tried to smile.

"What did they say?"

"Not much. Just accusations." She brought the words out in a series of breaths. "Corrupter." "Mind-fucker." "Murderer."

"Mada, for God's sake!"

"And then more messages while I was here in New York, even before I saw you. Things about you and others."

"Do you have one with you?" She took a folded piece of bond paper from her pocket. The watermark was clearly visible on the white vellum. It was in calligraphic script, a bastardization of the art form, for it said, "You're putting your mouth where cock has been. Your lovely Raquel lies."

"Mada . . . "

She squeezed my hand hard. "I was so happy that day when I got back to my apartment. Do you remember, my darling, the day we were here in the Cloisters?"

"Yes."

"I was so happy, you can't imagine. So happy finally to hear those words of love. I'll remember that always."

"It was only the first time. Believe it, Mada."

This time she smiled. I moved to kiss her, but she stopped me. "I have to tell you the rest, later it might be too hard." I held her hands and waited.

"The agents came. They said they'd received certain information about my `sexual' activities. What information? I asked them. They said it had to do with lesbian prostitution and other criminal acts, which they described to me in detail."

"Rush did that, didn't he?"

She nodded. "And then they said they were watching you and me, that they'd been watching us for some time, not only here but in California too, and that they had to assume you were involved."

"Those scum! Did they tell you not to see me anymore?"

"They said if we're together, we're both guilty."

"What does Ricard have to say about all that?"

"He's outraged, of course."

"Threatening to sue the government for slander, no doubt? But he wouldn't be too sorry if you couldn't see me."

"Raquel . . ."

"Mada, has it occurred to you that Ricard might be involved in these persecution tactics?"

Pain then disbelief crossed her face. "He's done . . . terrible things. He's beyond reason at times, but he'd never do that to me. I can't believe it."

"Mada, federal agents don't use bond paper and I doubt if they care what's been in the vaginas of the women you love. Or even who you love." Even as I said the words, I wondered.

"But those messages — surely they came from whoever is giving them that false information."

"I think it's all coming from the same source — your ever-loving husband Ricard."

"But the agents?"

Then I told her what else I'd been doing between

making all those phone calls to her apartment. Having run into the feds during my undergraduate political days, I'd known enough to try to contact them this time. They had been guarded, but I knew.

"There are no agents White and Rush operating in New York," I said. "And there's no von Brecht case, at least not yet."

It was hard for Mada to believe me. Like many people, she feared the authorities. After the 1950s and all the red-baiting since then, I guess she had good reason to be afraid. But there was something else to think about.

"They may not be who they say they are." I told her, "but who they are is bad enough. I think we should take their threats seriously."

She started to say something, but I stopped her. "And that doesn't mean not seeing you. I'll spit in the devil's eye if I have to. Nobody's pushing me away from you again."

Huddled in that dark corner, our teeth chattering from the cold, it was hard to be brave, but it was a promise I'd made to myself. When we could we went inside. The warm air was ambrosia. We held hands in the shadows and I told her softly, "If I can't hold you very soon, I'm going to go berserk with frustration and do something that they *will* arrest us for."

"That's what I like to hear," she said.

The old challenge was in her eyes. Tenderness made pleasure rise in my blood as I tightened my grip on her fingers. When I looked at her again, her eyes were closed, her lips slightly open. I thought of all the times I'd held this wonderful woman in my arms, nothing but the sweat of love between us, the times I'd taken her lips in my teeth, devouring her. And now it seemed like I had been waiting forever to feel her skin and taste her. She felt it and answered, then became a tigress, ready to spring. Now certain of her prey, she stretched out, waiting for the inevitable steps that would bring us together. But once we were outside again, Mada's fear returned and she insisted on parting. Tomorrow night I would be one of a crowd, and we would meet again after her performance.

    I hated abandoning my one suitcase, but that night I packed everything I had into a backpack and walked nonchalantly over to 11th Street. A blizzard had settled in off the Long Island coast. The city lay suspended under the threat of a storm as people attended to necessary last-minute tasks. There was a nervous feel to their movements and I was glad to get out of the way for a while in Bradley's, an NYU haunt good for a beer and the address of a place safe to stay for the night.

    There was even an ironing board in the flat and I used it to touch up the outfit I'd bought at the Sak's outlet on Second Avenue; black slacks and jacket, a tuxedo shirt, black walking boots and a grey overcoat, cut English-style. I slept, woke up, ate and slept again. I showered and dressed, left a twenty-dollar bill tacked to the bulletin board and went out to the rental car I'd had delivered earlier in the day, a nondescript compact. It was easy to squeeze into a corner space not far from the theatre. As I

Mada

walked towards the bright lights, the feelings I'd had for Mada since the beginning beat in my breast in a steady current of deep and abiding love, growing into a massive energy surge and lighting me up like a thousand coloured lights.

CHAPTER 9

THEATRE MNASIDIKA WAS A WOMEN'S ACTING COLLECtive that survived from production to production on donations. Emerging feminist theories of art were drawing some distinct lines, but the divisions seemed to lose meaning that night. Mada's benefit performance had pulled in a large and varied audience; uptown people in evening dress, academic faculty and students from Columbia, NYU and other schools and, of course, theatre people from the Village. The theatre was a large old building with high ceilings and a balcony running the length of three walls. The audience was on the same level as the performing area and the set design was a simple matter of grey rectangles and several living trees.

As the house lights dimmed, the old excitement of performance gripped me. A single blue spotlight came up, turning Mada's head into blue fire. Her hands slowly parted from her face and the first words of Rilke's *Eranna*

Mada

to Sappho burst into the clear light of our consciousness.

O du wilde weite werfein, O you fierce, far-flinging hunter! And then Sappho answering, *I want to flood you with unrest . . .* Speaking first in German, then in English, the elastic strength of her voice infusing every syllable with feeling, hurled us beyond Rilke's vision to a place that was hers alone. Each line rang resplendent, cast in the darkness of her womb. As she spoke, we raided eternity, stealing the essence from each word. She shed herself, layer by layer, to reveal the core of a vision clinging to me like the scent I carried away on my skin after touching hers.

I had known Mada the artist when I was very young and I had known the woman as my lover. Now the two came together in my heart for the first time in *I Could Not Wait: Yesterday you/ Came to my house/ And sang to me./ Now I/ Come to you./ Talk to me. Do./Lavish on me/ Your own beauty.*

Each sound was a note of music to Sappho's words as Mada played me with fingers of delight — *I See It Still and Feel It: . . . passion, yes/. . .utterly/ . . . I can./ . . . shall be to me/ . . . a face/. . . shining back to me/ . . . beautiful/ . . indelibly.*

When she'd finished, her hands, mouth, tears were inside me, our breath mingling, planting her trust in our so-mortal dreams. I was just one among many, going wild with ecstasy and pulling down the walls with applause. She was small, so small, yet tall and so great with beauty. We thrust our desperation aside and draped her in garlands of appreciation. Real flowers were thrown at her feet and bouquets laid in her arms by several women from the theatre collective, and then the space was a milling tangle of people as the audience began to disperse.

Admirers crowded around her, but this time I waited in the background by choice. I rejoiced at all she was given — how small our tribute compared to her gift to us. I waited. I watched and when I saw a moment I came close. Our eyes met. In that second between us it was as if our faces burned, her tear-stained cheeks, a child's lucid and pure countenance with ancient eyes, probed mine. Then a new group of elegantly clad bodies closed in around her and Ricard's tanned, sweating face bent towards me. A stale smile, his usual aplomb and the expensive odour of Ralph Lauren.

"And how is our lovely Raquel tonight?"

"Lovely and rough," I said. "Don't forget the rough. And I think the `our' is rather over-stated."

A strange mix of jealousy and glee flared in his eyes, backed by something I couldn't understand. His fingers closed on my shoulder. I hadn't realized before what a strong man he was.

Before I could not so subtly pull away from him, he said, "You'll come to our little party, won't you? As a special service to my wife, of course."

Everything the man said sounded obscene to me and he always referred to Mada in the same possessive way. I wondered what kind of fantasy life he had, but I tossed that thought away as too distasteful and asked where.

He stretched his lips again and handed me a folded

sheet of paper, with a side-long glance that suggested he and I were colluding in some evil. After he turned away, I checked the paper for watermarks, but there was only an address off Riverside Drive, not too far away.

I killed some time, found the building, took a private elevator to the top floor. The doors opened soundlessly onto a foyer decorated with Renaissance drawings that could have been originals, a formidable contrast of ages with the beautiful Black woman in neck-high leather who offered to take my overcoat. I kept it. The woman's radiant smile was only the beginning: her eyes were fantastic and warm, her fingers linked mine lightly but with a promise of intimacy that I felt in my thighs and the pit of my stomach.

She walked with me to the entrance of the penthouse and opened the door for me. I was in darkness that fell away into glass and the lights of the city. Islands of diamonds lay bare to our discretion and our lust — a body that could come no closer but whose being and desire pulled at our sex with offerings of pleasure. I knew the others felt it too. I watched people in evening dress moving like delicious shadows among muted red, blue and purple lights. The white ties of the men glowed like ice and the women's jewellery gleamed steel as they turned, silk and satin rubbing against each other and the legs of the men in an elaborate, silent dance.

Then floor, ceiling and vast walls began to undulate with figures. At first their size and proximity overwhelmed me. But then my eyes drowned in the liquid movements of her body, covering me like oil, drenching me in the heat of eternally reaching, anticipating orgasm.

"Raquel!" Her heated voice, her lips on my face, my neck, her hand taking me to a bed where we faced each other behind a wall of tinted glass.

Before I yielded, I had to know. "Why, Mada?"

She caressed me with her eyes and I unfolded, aching desire turning me to liquid mercury beneath the magnets of her fingers. She spoke with sadness.

"Because, my darling, I won't be made ordinary by your love."

The question remained in her eyes, her hand halted on the first button of my shirt. "If this were the only way you could have me?"

I nodded that I understood but asked her in return, "Then will you do what I ask?"

Her lips answered and she began to open my shirt. Kissing, coming together and breaking away in brief and intense touches, pleasure ignited me, causing me to widen and widen with the rushing sound of flame until my bodily senses knew the opening through which a universe poured an ancient dragon with greenblack eyes, eyes, blazing fire, drinking our nectar, act of art by virtue of audience.

After, dressed and carrying her stockings and shoes, my overcoat around her, I took her hand and brought her with me. In the hour before the snow descended on Manhattan, the plane we boarded took off from Kennedy. We rose above the battling storm, flung cleanly and smoothly, skating past the vast, silent blackness and into the stars.

CHAPTER 10

*T*HE HOT, FERTILE BACK ALLEYS OF NEW YORK CITY SEEM *to have no end. He is leading me deeper and deeper into the darkness and the alley narrows as the cobblestones gleam wetly and the walls rise smoothly upward. The narrowest of passageways is just visible as the darkness advances to the end. That much is known as I follow Ricard, with no desire and no thought but to keep going where he leads me to something I must see.*

I follow willingly, without rancour or distaste. At last the total darkness of the path ends at a small bright window. I see beautiful women, beautiful Mada, inviting me to join a spectacle of bodies at the far end of an otherwise empty room. The women move fluidly in a silent, flowing homage to Mada and to women touching women, to limbs and fingers, to colour and texture. She wants me there, watching, knows my ultimate act of love is to free her from all sense of possession and give her to the pleasure of others. I remove my last thought from her body and fling our souls into the silence, into that innermost sacred ecstasy where we are particles in a spontaneous configuration, remembering everything.

I am remembering this dream of the night before as I follow Mada through the dense snow. In the pure, frozen North, the earth keeps its own counsel. The modest home my mother had preferred to live in after my father's death and until her own, two years ago, borders several thousand acres of reserves. Geese and other waterfowl, caribou and deer roam in peace there. Now in winter the land lay cold beneath a windswept sky brushed along the horizon with deep green fur.

Mada and I had been walking all morning. We had gone far beyond the end of the road to a place where two rivers met. We climbed above the cracking sounds of water and ice, on a deer trail that hugged the mountain into a small glade covered with silver aspen. A roof of golden leaves, heavy with snow, rose above our heads as thick layers of leaves muffled our footsteps. Deeper and deeper we went, driven towards the centre of things as the air around us grew light and rare. I tried to tell her what had happened to me in the penthouse in New York and to answer her questions.

"Why wasn't it obscene, my darling?"

I could answer freely. "Because my love for you burst my dream of you. The entire world could see it without altering anything." I recalled others watching, sharing, as though I had stretched to include every human thought and gesture. Suddenly I was afraid.

"It can never happen like that again."

"Are you afraid for yourself?" she asked.

"And for you."

"But I know what's inside and what's external." She came towards me, but I pulled back from her.

"But I don't, Mada. Can't you see? You've taken me places I wouldn't have gone but for loving you. Of myself, I don't expect the unearthly. I'm only good at placing one foot in front of the other."

Her eyes flashed. "When we made love that night, was that on your earth?" I felt myself sinking away from her, a feather now become a rock. She let me go with her eyes and then I became more afraid.

"There are rules," I said.

"Yes, my dear Raquel. There are rules. Even I must suffer for breaking them." Her eyes held that haunted look from the morning at the Cloisters and I wanted to take away the hurt because her innocence was worth so much to me.

But instead I said, "Did Ricard have something to do with what we did?"

She smiled faintly. "You must know by now, Raquel, that he feeds my hunger. What he keeps for himself, I don't want to know."

"You gave in because of him."

"Not for him. For me." Her voice was one more whisper among the trees, her face lovely in partial concealment among the branches. My voice followed her, unnaturally loud.

"For what, Mada? For what?" And she told me again that she would not be made ordinary by our love.

"You would make our love — this love you say is your life — a matter of slices of toast served on matching plates. You would kill our love with devotion to clocks."

"I need to see you more often than every few months. What's wrong with that? Do I have to commit acts outside civilization to prove my feelings? Do I have to be willing to violate my own sense of the world?"

"How do you think I give my audiences so much?"

"We're not talking about the same thing. I'm talking about sex, about our bodies touching, about making love in the most intimate way possible, in total openness." I was already despairing.

"We are talking about the same thing."

"Why does it have to be that way? Why does it have to be great art for you to be happy? What ever happened to two people having a normal sex life?"

The leaves rustled as she broke into laughter and I laughed too. Then she said seriously, "Do you believe I'd be like this with anyone?"

"Yes, that's exactly what I think. With anybody you desire."

Her move and my response were inevitable. "This is my love for you," she said and reached inside my coat, inside my trousers, her fingers parting my pubic hair, pressing against my knot of sex, her face caressing mine,

Mada

our heat mixing together. Then she took her hand away and put it to her mouth. Her eyes closed, she licked her fingers then put her lips on mine, her tongue in my mouth. The flavour of our souls lingering in my mouth, inside my heart, taste for taste, was everything I wanted to be. "I give you everything!" she said.

When I took my mouth away from her I held her face with both hands. "When we leave here, I'm going back to the west coast. I want to know if you're coming too. I want to know if you'll live part of your life with me. You don't have to drink tea with me in the morning, I don't care. Our life together can be sweet and peaceful, and maybe it will feed you too. Maybe it will give you something you need for the parts of your life I can't share. I want to have all we can have. I'm asking you to try, for me. Because I can't bear uncertainty. I must have you."

She wouldn't tell me what she was thinking or feeling and I couldn't imagine. Tears were in her eyes, but I held her. I wouldn't let her walk away, not even when sobs shook her body. I held her and kept her looking at me, made her tell me with her very tears what I was to her. Our kisses tasted of salt, but their sweetness drained my fear and as she walked far ahead of me and out of sight, back towards the house, I was content. But when I reached her at the door, she said, "I won't let greed ruin our love."

"My greed? Or your lack of it?" I knew the words to be false as soon as I said them. Close to bitterness she said, "If I weren't the way I am, you wouldn't have me now."

"It's the only way I can have power with you."

"Why do you need that?"

"Because you have me body and soul. There's nothing I am that I wouldn't give you."

Again a trace of bitterness showed around her mouth. "I know you think that's true. I believe that you think it's important."

"Love for you begins and ends in bed."

"My darling . . ."

It was the first time she had stopped herself from telling me something and it scared me. But I was immersed in the perversity of what I felt. I would rather not have known what I was capable of, rather not have known that desperation and need to possess. Even that was her gift to me. I wanted her the way she wanted herself. I was the one obsessed. I wanted to break into her dreams of herself, didn't care what I destroyed in the process. My fingers were trembling when I took them away from her face.

"What is it, my darling?" But I couldn't — wouldn't — tell her. I knew if I hurt her there, our love would be finished. And then that feeling passed.

"I don't want anything."

She turned to me anyway, offering, trying, but I was cold. I don't know how I slept, but the next morning I was up before her. It was snowing, but not even the snow could cleanse me of what I felt. I couldn't walk and stood for hours, staring out the window. And when I went outside, the cold could not burn out my ugliness. Afterward, I went inside and played Vivaldi, his contained frenzy the

Mada

only music I could stand.

Each precious day passed. We let them go without marking them, fearful of the time ending, unable to stop or alter it.

One day I searched around in the garage and pulled out my old brushes and paints. She sat for me in front of the fire and let me work, watching the logs burn as I studied her. She never asked to see what I was doing, but each day a terrible something began to dissolve within me.

I cut and sliced her face on the canvas. It was my father's pathology. I understood his fixation with sharp edges, scalpels, the tools of his profession. When he was alive we never spoke after our first words of greeting. He sickened me with his knives, the way he cut his meat with the same precision and dexterity I imagined he used as he sliced his corpses for autopsy. I saw those feelings come out of me in yellows and reds, gnarled masses of purple and green. I smoothed away the blood and tissue, erased the haemorrhaging wounds. I made them flesh and separated myself from my father.

Mada sat for me through it all, available to me. And she brought my mother back to me. Bred from generations of subservient women, I had detested her slavery to my father. I remembered how she had been around the house when I was growing up, a silent shadow there to serve, remembered how I had come to visit and she had made a place for me without asking anything. She had let me be and I had barely acknowledged her.

I painted Mada's beautiful face the way it really was,

with the glow of her skin, the alertness in the eyes. Her hands falling loosely over the arms of the chair were the hands that had given me so much pleasure, hands that knew me more intimately than anyone had known me. In the vulnerability and strength of Mada's body, I recaptured my mother's strength. The last time I had embraced my mother, I had held her small body in my arms for only a moment. Now I knew that what I had felt running through her even as she lay dying was her love for me. It had always been there. How else could she have lived with my father and me, lived with our rejection? Now for the first time in my life I wanted to be like her and it was too late to tell her.

But perhaps she knew. I felt her coming into the room, asking to see my painting, discovering in myself that I wanted her to. She told me what I already knew, how beautiful Mada was. It was possible for pain to end. All along I had been looking at this truth in her face, but I hadn't seen it. I had only seen the surface, mesmerized by my attraction to her but never knowing its origin. And she had seen me so easily, had tried countless times to tell me. Her laughter, her brightness, her exquisite touching of me was all because of it.

I washed my brushes, cleaned up the mess in the bathroom and threw away the stained rags. I looked at the painting alone for a long time and then I went to the bedroom to find Mada.

She lay motionless on her bed, holding a book between hands as tenderly as orange blossoms at midnight cling to their bough. Because of the darkness I had embraced and loved in myself I now could see the contrast in her eyes, dark blue aureoles circling green pupils. The darkness in her eyes was the stuff of magic, necessary and vital. She raised her eyes to mine and held me there, wanting to sip at her pool of memory and then rise from her black waters, pale and newborn, with skin as fragile as lace. She held me until I broke through my flesh and flooded her with heat, then turned to me, yielding hands and body, taking mine entirely. How I had missed the relinquishing anguish of our embrace, the beauty we made from chaos and confusion.

Unclothed, her ass, her thighs, her breasts moved beneath a river of green water, where I dove again and again into the source. "Raquel!" she said once, sounding my name as it had never been spoken before. And I heard the passion in her voice echo deep in my soul just as I had longed to touch her life, to bring it to my lips and feel her fingers entwined in perfect knowledge of my need.

CHAPTER 11

THE NEXT DAY WAS THE 23RD OF DECEMBER. I IDLED THE jeep for an hour and drove us to town. On the way we skirted lake waters, vast and grey, so different in their tension from the free Pacific. In town the snow was piled high at the intersections, giving access to the baker, the meat market, the variety store and the post office.

In front of the feed store a caribou sleigh gave rides to children. Mada wandered off in that direction as I went about the business of buying provisions for the week. Many of the locals recognised me, asked after my health and how my life was in California. They were pleased to see me, reminding me of my mother by saying the holidays were a good time to come home. It was strange. I didn't know why I kept coming back, why I hung on to the old house, except that the North was in my blood. I had come to know myself in its clean, cold reaches and in its

Mada

trees, animals and waters, where the sun-tarnished sky reflected itself copper and red. When I arrived at the feed store I was surprised to find Mada there in conversation with Mr. Bergel. But they were both German, so they had things to talk about.

"Where did you find her?" he asked me. I could only smile.

"We met many years ago," Mada said. "When Raquel was a very young student." She turned my heart over with that and she knew it.

"Our Raquel. Such a smart scholar and such a traveller she is," said Mr. Bergel.

"But I always come back," I said. The old man agreed.

"To let us see how well she's doing. But you must make her some knudel and roast beef. And some strudel," he told Mada. "She's been studying too hard — she's all bones."

He tsk-tsked, pressing my arm and shaking his head. The idea of Mada in the kitchen making strudel amused me. But she said, "With delicious apples, mien herr," and they picked out walnuts, raisins, cinnamon and reddish-gold winesnaps and piled them on the counter, commenting in German on the quality of each item. When Mr. Bergel wasn't looking, Mada winked at me. I was suddenly shy and humbled by their kindness. We were just preparing to leave when a small boy ran in, carrying a bundle in his arms. He carefully unwrapped it to show us, his blue eyes on the verge of tears.

Mada

A grey and white pet rat, with the dull, expressionless eyes of a severely injured animal lay on the towel. The rat's leg had been bitten by a cat and the flesh lay open in more than one place. Mr. Bergel brought cotton and disinfectant, but Mada stopped him and asked for water and sugar. She mixed a solution and dropped some into the rat's mouth. The animal immediately wriggled and tried to stand. While Mr. Bergel held him steady Mada cleaned the wounds and put ointment on them. When bandaged the rat tried to bury his head in Mada's bosom and she stroked him gently until he quieted. Then she wrapped him carefully in the towel and gave him to the boy with instructions for home care. Mr. Bergel, plainly in love with Mada now, said something in German I couldn't understand and went to get some schnapps. We drank to each other's health and to St. Nicholas.

"Are you ready to go home?" I asked her outside.

"One more thing, my darling." We put our packages in the jeep and she took my arm and steered me back to the caribou sleigh. The children had gone and the owner was amenable to letting us take the sleigh for a small fee. Mada surprised me again by taking the double reins expertly in her hands, urging the caribou onto the road. We trotted past the town church, decked with Christmas lights on the hill, and turned into hushed, snow-covered woods. The sleigh bells rang above the whooshing of the runners passing over the snow as the large, many-pointed antlers of the caribou sailed before us. Timelessness enveloped us as all around great, snow-laden trees rose, and beneath them smaller trees, lushly green and new. Mada stopped the sleigh by a clearing and the caribou stood stolidly, at home in the winter landscape. For the first time I thought I saw a little blue in the green of her eyes.

"When I was a little girl," she said, "every year at Christmas time we went to the Black Forest. The elk and the caribou ran in herds then."

Mada got down from the sleigh and walked a little way into the snowy field, towards the trees on the other side. "My mother was always finding wounded animals who needed our care and bringing them home to nurse." I started to follow her, but she ran from me. She turned and called, "My brother Ralf found a small hare in a farmer's trap and gave it to me in a box he'd made from pine branches."

I watched her tramp into the woods and stand among the trees, looking up. I went back to the sleigh, saw the sky become a red rush behind the trees and waited.

We didn't speak on the way to town or on the ride home. We could no longer see the water; it was too dark. The only thing visible was snow in the headlights of the jeep. I carried the packages to the kitchen table, then built a fire from the coals left from the afternoon. I checked the thermometer; it was already ten below and dropping. I brought a large supply of wood into the house, stacking it by the fireplace. Since coming home, Mada had been sitting in the armchair, the chair she sat in while I painted, but now it seemed somehow too big for her. The fire burned warmly. I asked to take her coat, which she gave me. It was the overcoat she had worn when we left New York.

She looked up at me. I couldn't tell what she was thinking. Then she said, "When two people are together too long, sooner or later, miene liebe, it comes."

"What comes, Mada?" I stood before her, holding the overcoat.

"The stories of our life. We can't escape it."

"It's acceptable to share personal history."

"No, Raquel. We try to make the dead live, but they cannot. They cannot live."

"If it's what's in your heart, Mada, it's okay to let it out."

She sighed deeply and touched my face with a cold hand.

"No. We're the ones who're made to taste death, my darling." I held her hand, tried to kiss her. She wouldn't let me.

"I can't feel. Can't love at a time like this," she said.

"I can feel for both of us," I said. "I can love for both of us. As long as you need me to. And I will." I kissed her hands, made them warm with my breath. I could feel her trembling.

"And when we have to leave each other — look at me — when I have to return to my life and you to yours what happens to our love then?"

"It lives. Even when I can't see you, I don't stop thinking of you. I don't stop feeling you."

"And when you decide there are limits to our love,

what will happen to me then?"

"All I can tell you is what I feel right now — that I know enough to ask you to reschedule your life, damn it, and be in mine. For whatever time you can be in California, stay with me. See me. You can take the time you need to do your work up there in the cabin."

She loosened my grip on her hands, saying passionately, "I've lived alone too long, Raquel."

"It's not too late."

"Believe me. These moments together are gifts from heaven. There's nothing more."

"Just say you'll try it."

"That's the point, Raquel. I don't want to try what I'm sure must fail." She stood up and pushed past me to stand in front of the fire.

"What's the worst that can happen, Mada? That I won't like the amount of toilet paper you use? Or you won't like my habit of never eating leftovers? It doesn't have to rest on those things."

"It doesn't. We are much more; each other's food and drink. We are excessive."

"I'll learn to take smaller bites."

"And me?" She didn't wait for an answer. "The time we're away from each other is necessary."

"All right! I know that. But I just need to know if and when I'll see you again. I need to be able to count on it." I stood beside her. "Don't say anymore now, please. Wait. Keep thinking about it. Okay?

Finally, she nodded. I tossed her coat towards the

clothes tree. "And anyway, where's that strudel you make so well?"

"Ya, ya, the strudel," she laughed.

I touched her softly. "You need me too."

"Raquel . . . " I kissed away the words from her mouth.

The next night we ran lights out to the fir tree by the window. Mada proved to be quite adept at untangling the mess of cords. With a pang I remembered that my mother had always been the patient one — my father and I throwing on the tinsel and the coloured balls, all the fun stuff, while my mother got the practical job of unpacking the ornaments. But she was the one who hung the angel at the top of the tree. I found it at the bottom of a box filled with fake candy canes. One wing was coming off, but I fixed it with glue and left it to bond while Mada and I connected the extension cords.

"Yes!" we shouted. "Yes, yes!" when the last plug was in and a spectrum of coloured light fanned out over the snow. I walked away from the house a hundred yards and waved Mada to me. We stood together, admiring the spectacle.

"The angel, my darling. You've forgotten her."

"Let's do it together." I brought the angel out tenderly and held on to the stool while Mada climbed up and stretched her arms, planting the angel with her radiating halo at the top of the tree. We looked at everything from a distance again. It was perfect. The angel's great feathered wings were a golden lustre of light and the halo reached out to us through the darkness. I turned Mada's face to mine, touched her lips with my lips and remembered the kiss that had sealed our love. It already seemed so long ago but had been only a few weeks. I wanted to but didn't ask for promises. Holding her in my arms made a circle of completeness that absorbed all my doubts and freed my pleasure in one sweet motion.

The temperature Christmas morning was 23 below. True to her word, Mada made the best and only apple strudel I had ever eaten. And indeed, we were both feeling on the heavy side after our Christmas Day meal of turkey, sweet potatoes, corn and dessert. We snoozed the afternoon away in front of the fire, listening to music and making forays to the kitchen for another delicious tidbit or two. I felt young and free, and Mada's relaxed and smiling face and her sleepy embraces told me she felt that way too. She made the house a home for me, and I think she too had begun to feel a little of the safety and security I had intended by bringing her there.

The sun never really came out that day, and towards evening the temperature rose slightly and large, fluffy wet snowflakes descended once more. We went outside and by the light of the tree traded some snowballs. Her's were spectacularly well-aimed, but I was the winner in the wrestling match to put snow down each other's necks. We were splendidly winded and still hiccuping from laughter when Mada collapsed on the sofa and I began picking up refuse and straightening the room. I was gathering all the stray paper I could find to burn in the fire when I picked up what I thought was an envelope of some kind from the floor near the clothes tree. It came open in my hand. At first I didn't know what I was seeing, and then a depraved and vengeful world came crashing down on me. Mada looking up, saw my face and what I was holding. She came and took the photographs from my hands.

CHAPTER 12

"IS THIS THE REASON FOR THE THREE-RING CIRCUS IN New York?" My voice sounded harsh and wired. For a moment it seemed like she wouldn't say anything, but then she simply said no.

It wasn't enough for me. I took the pictures away from her: one of me, one of her. Again the same voice, the same kind of question. "Did you want me that way because you believed this?"

I held the images aloft, black and white on matt paper, technically close to perfect but torn where the folds had been and there was a line through Ricard's genitals and my face.

"No." It came from deep inside of her.

I was merciless. "Or because he threatened you with this?

I held up the other photo: Mada surrounded by

Mada

young girls with their fingers in places they shouldn't have even known about. My heart was pounding like a hurdles runner in a dead heat. What I saw was enough like my dream to make the blood rush from my brain. In the terror of the moment I saw my own hidden desires and fantasies mirrored in the photo and the extent to which I — or anyone — could go if self-control were not exercised. And though she didn't need to hear it from me I had to ask her if it were true. I had to know to wrest the beast from myself.

Only her eyes moved in her face. "No." She continued. "He tried to persuade me with that one — the one of me with Ricard — and to threaten me with this one — the one of her." She blanched then and looked like she might fall but regained her strength, waiting for me to say it.

"Would you — did you — sacrifice me to them?"

"Never."

"Were you giving me a choice of depravities? Theirs or yours?"

"Raquel!" Her first real anger at me was a hot white flame that seared my illusions but left the better part standing.

"I know my own desires — and yours — this is what we are!" She didn't touch me but took me with her eyes and my thighs tightened until I exploded outward. In that moment of intense physical response I knew what I had to know and I made my decision. I pulled her to me. She pressed against me, moans coming from her throat, our bodies shattering, then fused and charged with fire.

Later she said, "I can't believe he did this."

"Not alone," I said. "Not him alone." I picked up the photos from the floor where they had fallen.

"We've already paid for these pictures."

"Yes." I got my briefcase, packed the photos in a folder with the obscene calligraphic note she had given me and relocked the case.

"I'm going to San Francisco tonight. I have to."

She was already nodding. "There's something else, Raquel." She took a key from her bag and gave it to me.

"After Midge died, a box came for me. I didn't look closely at the contents, but there were negatives and other things."

I took the key from her hand. "Will you wait here for me?"

"How long?"

"Tomorrow, three days to get there, another to return — I'll be back in less than a week."

"I'll wait."

"You're safe here. Do you know that now? Even without me, the place will take care of you." She kissed me.

I left her the jeep. It was Christmas night and traffic was sparse. A cab took me to a car rental agency in the next town and I drove the several hours to Minneapolis-St. Paul easily. The midnight plane to San Francisco was full, however, and I waited on stand-by, biting my fingernails and hoping each last-minute arrival wouldn't take the last seat. I got on, the harried stewardess carrying my bag for me, pushing me and it into the plane without ceremony, sealing the door after us. When the plane rose into the night I looked beyond the lights of the Twin Cities into the darkness of the North. I reached out to touch Mada, hold her to me, sense her tenderness and strength. Then I could sleep.

Early morning Market Street, tired and littered with Christmas garbage and depleted stores. The morning-after emptiness would soon fill with shoppers eager to glean a last leftover bargain. I found the U-Rent storage Mada's key fit and a hotel nearby where I got a room and a shower. Then I sat in a businessmen's luncheonette, eating breakfast and waiting for the U-Rent to open. Finally it was time and I got Midge's box, a medium-sized cardboard box on the heavy side, and carried it up to my hotel room. I started going through it.

Old negatives and photographs, things I remembered and times I hadn't known about. Ways of looking at bodies I hadn't known Midge possessed. I could tell when the work became more recent — delayed action photos of Mada, informal poses possibly taken without her knowing, probably in hotel rooms. Then some surprisingly candid photos of me when the camera had to have been on a timer. In the high contrast, of the whites and blacks on certain areas of the body and its attitudes, I began to see the formal constructions of the work that had peaked in the retrospective.

I didn't know what I was looking for, but I examined everything in the box. At the bottom lay a box of unexposed 11 by 16 inch photographic paper. I lifted a corner of the lid, saw the silver foiled corners within and retaped the lid. I put everything back in the box and lay down on the bed to think. But jet lag caught up with me and I slept. I dreamed about bodies: mine, Mada's, Midge's, in a whirling dance in which we turned and turned and changed in our turning into beams of light. Then I saw Ricard and a shadowy figure in monk's garb, putting pen to paper.

I woke to the late afternoon sunlight reaching in beneath the window shade and warming my breasts. I mentally calculated the time difference and tried to call Mada, but there was no answer. The answering machine wasn't on either. I gave up, got my briefcase and went downstairs to the camped-up scene on lower Market Street. I took a trolley, clutching a bar as I stood on the crowded step, the wind whipping up from the Bay. I rode to Jackson Street and walked over to Chinatown from there. Passing the theatre, I saw a Kurasawa film was playing and regretted not being able to take the time to go in. I shouldered past the tourists, past the fancy neon-lit restaurants that catered to those with money to spend.

All the little knick-knack stores were open. No pressure now. Nobody trying very hard to sell or to buy anything. Just walkers ambling along, satiated by the holidays. A place I call the One-Ton Sloop was open. Ship's emblem on the door, a spoked wheel. A funny choice, I had thought, for a chopstick place, until I got to know the owner and found out he had been a battleship commander in the Second World War. He was also a Chinese master in the Zen tradition and that's why I wanted to see him.

Mada

My former teacher, Jerry Liu, in a black suit and a clean white apron and looking older, was serving rice to a customer. When he saw me we bowed formally to each other, then a big smile creased his face.

"Raquel, long time no see!" He ushered me to an out-of-the-way table and summoned a boy over and told him to bring cashew duck and plenty of rice wine.

"Thanks, Jerry, but not tonight. Just vegetables and plain rice. I have to stay clear."

He was immediately helpful. "Sit. Eat. Then I'll come back and we'll talk."

I enjoyed the food like I always had, using the chopsticks to pick up one grain at a time. My teacher's words came back to me: "One grain, ten thousand grains." The spiritual and material worlds in harmony. Actions and their consequences: the inexorable laws of the universe, beyond good or evil. Yin and yang. Order on a human scale. When Jerry came back the dinner crowd had gone and we could talk freely. He took off his apron, examined me with bright eyes in a round, serene face. I saw how age was taking the fullness from his body, but it was good to feel that clarity in his presence again, to see him measuring me with his eyes and to see that I was acceptable. Or perhaps he did no measuring, just saw through to the essence.

"I need your help, Jerry. I need to know something. This paper I'm going to show you — don't ask about what it says, okay? Just look at it and tell me what I need to know."

He nodded, took the folded sheet from my hand, studied the letters. I watched his face, but he showed no reaction.

"How can I help you, Raquel?"

"The calligraphy — it's origin. I need to know the school. Japanese?"

"No school," he said. "It's not Japanese."

Jerry never said anything unless he was sure.

"Self-taught, then?"

"Yes and no. With exposure to the Two Wangs tradition. You see this upward turn of the U? Certain Mandarin characters of that style always have this peculiar turn of the point of the brush."

"Is there a Two Wangs master here?"

"No master, but there are students."

"Where?"

"Try the Ashram on Haight Street, near the Park."

"That's all I need to know, Jerry. You've just confirmed something for me."

"Are you in trouble, Raquel?" His kind eyes almost made me want to tell all, but I still retained enough of my Zen training to keep myself from needlessly sullying the master's repose. He joined me in eating a last bowl of rice, the sound of our clicking chopsticks somehow soothing and invigorating me.

I went back to my hotel, took out the photos and the calligraphic note. The small brush strokes were beautiful, orderly, consistent — the kind of effortless flow achieved only in a state of meditation. But I had learned long ago

Mada

from Jerry Liu that we could choose to become angels or demons at any time — it's always a matter of choice. I leafed through the negatives in Midge's box again, wondering for the tenth time why she had chosen these photos to give Mada. Memories of good times when love was easy and painless? A record of the beginning of our triangle when things were clear and honest and desire was perfect? I didn't know. I decided to keep some of the negatives of Mada: if I couldn't sleep I could go to the all-night lab on Potrero and develop some prints. I took the photographic paper and the negatives and put them in my briefcase. Maybe it wasn't such an insane idea. Maybe it would bring me an hour of sanity in the midst of chasing shadows.

    The next day the City turned dreary and cold. I was glad for the thermal jacket I'd lugged west with me. I drove to Haight Street, and if I hadn't suddenly gotten a yen for flavours from the past, I wouldn't have gone into the Polish deli. I was waiting in line to order and idly looking out the display window at the Haight when I saw White and Rush.

    Same old trenchcoats doing double duty as raincoats in the drizzle now falling on the city. I left without the peroshki and ducked into the smoke shop at the corner to watch White and Rush climb the steps of a building on Masonic. Rush slipped going up; I could almost hear his foul mouth as White calmly elbowed him the rest of the way. I couldn't see who opened the door, but I didn't need to. Had they come for me? If so, why? I stood there, pretending to look at the hash pipes and admiring an assortment of silver, gold and jewelled coke spoons from a recent time that was already passing into history, when drug use was innocent. What serious user would buy that paraphernalia now? Tourists out for souvenirs? T-shirts from rock concerts of the 60s and framed front pages of the famous Oracle hung on the walls.

I roamed the store but kept an eye on the street. Just as I was running out of objects to look at I saw White and Rush slip and slide down the stairs and along the sidewalk, then jaywalk the corner and get into a Toyota that was obviously a rental. When the car pulled out I saw that the left rear bumper was smashed; either their luck was running wild, or one of them had a penchant for trying to elbow other vehicles out of the way. The car jerked away in the direction of Golden Gate Park. I waited a couple of minutes, then went over and rang Jake's bell. The look on his face when he saw me was nothing short of astonishment.

"God, Raquel."

"Yeah," I said. We spoke our greetings like well-rehearsed puppets, I wondered whose. I didn't wait for him to ask me in but pushed past him and stood in the doorway to the studio in shock. Boxes of photographs and negatives cluttered the floor and spilled over every piece of furniture.

"Moving?" I asked. "Inventory Day, is that it?"

Jake didn't look at me. Didn't say a word. Just brushed by me and sat down on a small black meditation cushion and clasped his hands together on the low table. Watching his gestures, I remembered the long afternoons of Shankar and Koto music and the scratch, scratch, scratching of Jake's bamboo pen as he practised his working meditation. I opened the briefcase, took out the folded sheet of bond paper and the photos and placed them in front of him. He swallowed but didn't pick them up. I sat down opposite him, arranged my legs in a half-lotus and waited. When he finally looked at me, a red flush had crept up his neck into his face, but the area around his eyes stayed pale and grey.

"She was ruining Midge's life," he said in a voice that had long ago cast off any self-doubt. "You were both doing it."

Suddenly I leaped to a place I didn't know was in me. "Is that why you made the pictures of me and Mada, Jake? To hasten Midge's disillusionment? To tear open her world, you fucking bastard?"

My words had no effect on him at all. My anger changed briefly to fear as I saw his knuckles whiten, but that too passed. A smile twisted his face.

"I'll never let Mada rest." His eyes said he meant me too.

"Don't forget Midge," I said. "Can she rest?"

His eyelids flickered, but he hung on. "She could have been great."

"She was great."

"But she was hung up on being Mada's dyke lover — it was sucking the life out of her."

"Midge lived her own life."

"Mada was warping her soul, making her do things. She could have done stuff that was real."

"Women with women, bodies of women loving one another — it wasn't Mada. It wasn't even me. Midge didn't find out what she really wanted, didn't find out how to do it until you showed her, did she, Jake?" His eyes stopped tracking whatever it was, came back to mine, struggled to stay there.

"She could have gotten over losing Mada, but then you came around, telling your lies."

"How did I lie, Jake?"

"You acted like you cared, then . . ."

"I wasn't acting. I did care. But I was trying to be something to her I couldn't be. And you're right, Midge made me realize it."

He sounded tired. "You didn't even want her."

"No. I did want her, I just didn't know how to deal with wanting her. I knew that I would always be at the edge of Mada's life, waiting for her."

He winced as I said those last words but stayed silent, barely breathing. I looked around the room. Had those good and happy times really happened? Had we really lived here, loved here? Did Midge live on somewhere else, taking her golden light and her vision with her, leaving us to wrestle with our memories in the dark?

"What about Ricard?" I asked, trying to sound like I knew more than I did.

"Ricard." Bitterness and disgust in his voice. "He

couldn't pull anything off by himself. He has no ideas, no ability to think creatively."

I wasn't so sure of that, thinking of his settings for Mada and her lovers.

"Is that why he needed you, Jake?"

Again that slightly twisted smile, an inverse copy of Midge's, elation and dejection fighting for prominence in his eyes.

"Or did he only need you for the execution? So your hands would be on everything and he could remain safely in the background?"

His eyes scrambled over the disarray of negatives and photos on the floor, searching for something. "We wanted the same thing," he shrugged.

"Breaking up the three of us. But Midge fooled you, didn't she? She took her greatest inspiration from your mud and shit and made it beautiful."

He was shaking his head.

"She went places neither of you ever dreamed she'd go with your nasty lies. She took your betrayal of her and made it her greatest possibility, the tension that tied us together. Her, me, Mada — forever."

I was on a roll now, running in front of the fear in his eyes. "You almost broke her, but you know what? In the end the love and the wanting between us was all she still believed in. That's what you can't stand about the retrospective, isn't it?"

He shouted back at me, painfully, "She died because of the two of you!"

Mada

My grief dissolved. "No," I said quietly. "Not after the work she'd just produced. There's no way she could have killed herself." I felt tears fill my eyes and course down my cheeks.

"Bad drugs. I gave her what she wanted. Always tried to do what she wanted."

I found pity even for him in myself. His voice had become dull again, his body had no edge, no hope. I said, "We only knew the fun part of getting high; we never understood the psychic part, the uprooting of self, the way Midge did. We never had to find out how ugly it could get, how it could kill. She played it out for all of us."

Jake sat like a shrivelled old man now. I knew there would be no more pictures and no more letters. A tragic accident had taken Midge's life and if it hadn't happened when it did she would have made it through like the rest of us. I knew that now. I wiped my eyes and face and left Jake there.

Outside the rain had stopped. The streets glistening and clean, the air fresh. I got my peroshki and an apple-cinnamon yogurt and took them with me to the top of Potrero where I sat in the sun opening over the city and ate my lunch. San Francisco, the beautiful woman, looked lovely to me once again, but my love for her would always be a little bittersweet, just enough to remind me that love and happiness had a price I had agreed to pay. After I ate and said goodbye to the city, I went to the lab. I spent more time there than I had expected, but I developed some prints to take with me. Then I tied up loose ends and

Mada

drove to the airport. I checked in my rental car and confirmed a seat on the evening flight to Minneapolis. I called Mada, left a message when I'd be arriving and settled down in front of a TV until it was time to board the plane.

CHAPTER 13

I DIDN'T EXPECT MADA TO BE THERE, BUT SHE WAS WAITING for me when I landed in Minneapolis. The time difference made it late evening, but the strain of the past week and the revelations of my last day in San Francisco had taken their toll. Not even Mada's arms could keep me awake and I slept. I awakened like always at first light but buried my head under the pillow and went back to sleep. The slight clatter of dishes and smell of coffee woke me a second time. It was almost two in the afternoon, eleven o'clock in the morning California time. Mada, with strawberry jam on her breath, was buttering a piece of toast she said was mine. The eggs were still warm and I ate like I was starving.

Mada's green eyes studied me from time to time, but she refrained from asking me anything. Maybe I wanted to keep the glow of my return as long as I could. Maybe I wanted to delay deciding about the future. I didn't immediately tell her all I'd learned in San Francisco or what I'd found at the lab. Or maybe it was because her fingers began to touch me and my anxiety and pent-up desire rose to her touch. Her lips and teeth and tongue followed her hands over my body, burning past hidden resistance, eating me at last.

Crossing the bridge of our desire, she held me long enough to say, "This is my love for you," and then I broke to her and our separate lives fused in a perfect moment. Holding her in my arms, feeling the hollow at her waist, suspended me in memories of other times I had wanted her and reached for her in the unknown depths of beginnings without finding her. Here, where only naked, uncontrollable desire could live, I found her. Place of no shadows, burning in the ice-light squeezed from a star. I made my pleasure from the endless sources of her breasts and throat and thighs. My hands grew more silken with every stroke of her skin and I lost myself inside her flesh-become-water and fed at the green of her eyes. Then I put my body against hers, fit myself into its waves, until she turned solid again. Only then did we kiss mouth to mouth, untangle essence from essence and taste the last drop of our holy transgressions.

Without washing her scent off my body, I drove the miles back to the reserves with Mada beside me, hurtling by snow, past swollen icy streams, and the thick dark brushes of trees against the tarnished sky. The air became purple as night fell. My dependable jeep, that workhorse of desolate places, ran strong against a rocking wind and icy road. Nevertheless, it was a relief to see the cabin's light from a distance and to come upon its warmth and safety.

I slept as usual in my loft bed, but I got up twice to pad softly in stocking feet to stand beside her bed. Hearing her breathe, those soft puffs of sound as she exhaled, made me want to crawl into her dream. I wanted to feel through her senses that strange and mystical union of spirit winging beyond breath. I wanted to come upon myself in the dark and narrow street of total expectation, to tear my newborn self from her earth and find I could still bleed, wanted to keep my pleasure and my pain, my deliverance through lust.

Love had no body. As I stood near her I felt only the mystery. I longed to touch her again, to be that unearthly self, though now it seemed unnecessary. I admired the silence, the smell of her sleep, her perfumed journey. But suddenly I could no longer fathom my solitude and I took her in my arms just to feel that rush of love and desire that even in sleep flowed from her body into mine.

In the morning the light filtered warmly through the panes of stained-glass over my bed. I opened my eyes to see an intense blue sky and my spirits leapt at its promise.

"Were you here, my darling, last night?" she asked me.

"You didn't wake," I said. "Not even when I kissed you."

"It couldn't have been with passion then," she joked.

"Beyond passion, beyond memory. Beyond imagination."

"Hmm," she said, her eyes twinkling. Then she asked me seriously, "You're happy then, miene liebe?"

"Today roses will bloom in the midst of the snow. Today I don't have to go anywhere, find out any secrets, pay back any debts. I want to make cupcakes out of snow — no, that's child's play — I want us to make our lives into anything we want!"

"Achs." she replied. "Then feed me."

"In what way?" I touched her breast lightly with my fingertips, teasing, but she stuck a piece of slightly burned toast in my mouth.

"First, I must eat food. Then you."

"Promises," I laughed, setting the grill. I made buckwheat pancakes, which we ate covered with cranberry sauce left from Christmas, and an omelet with tiny bits of scallion, fresh mushrooms and tomatoes, a dish I'd learned to cook by living in California. Mada ground fresh coffee beans in a grinder I hadn't seen since my mother's death.

It all seemed so normal. I kept looking at her out of the corner of my eye until she said, "You're looking at me so strangely, Raquel. Have you eaten the wrong thing?" I couldn't tell if she was making fun of me or if she was serious. Unable to answer her, I said, "Would you like to go for a morning walk?"

Then she knew what I meant and answered with a face suddenly gone tired. "You take advantage."

"Mada . . ."

"You're right, of course. I won't die because the clock's hands mark our time together."

"I didn't mean it that way. Tell me you're not enjoying this?"

"You're a fine cook in many ways, Raquel. And I have a big appetite — I want too much of everything. Maybe that's why I impose discipline on myself. If I didn't I would soon get lost in the commonplace."

"You're the most uncommon person I've ever known," I said with passion.

A brief smile warmed her face. "But you can't guess, can you, what it takes for me to maintain my integrity?"

"I can! I can," I repeated more quietly. "And I won't take that away from you."

"Maybe you can't avoid it. Maybe no one can."

My exasperation got the better of me. "It's just a walk, a healthy walk outdoors. I'm not asking you to jump off a cliff." For a moment, I thought I had blown it completely, but she surprised me once again by laughing and when she kissed me, it meant more than any babble of words.

As we went outside the sun was sparkling on the snow. I carried the snowshoes in case we wanted to trek off-trail. Snowdrifts hung in blue shadows and the sheer whiteness of the morning drew us further into its embrace with each step. From the road's end I spied a doe and a buck moving leisurely on the hill above us. We buckled on our snowshoes and climbed to the treeline. Stopping to catch our breath, we looked down on the valley below. Swatches of musty brown and green stood out against the whiteness where pieces of forest cut across the hillside. To the northwest a thin stream of smoke from our home fire rose straight into the rose-coloured air. A scattering of squirrels chucked pine nuts in the tree above us and bits of pine cone fluff fell on our heads.

"Go to sleep!" I called to them. But pine fluff and nut shells continued falling in rhythm with their chattering, so we fled to a tamer pair of aspen. The feisty squirrels were dumping snow from the branches now, but as I looked upslope I glimpsed the soft, rusty body of the doe again, slipping mysteriously between the trees. I pointed and Mada nodded and then the deer showed herself in a small clearing between two pines. We drank in her loveliness; the silken splendour of her long-limbed body, her large expressive eyes as she turned her head and returned gaze for gaze before vanishing out of sight with one splendid leap. We were left with the impression of a dream. I turned to Mada, startled by her intake of breath and saw tears in her eyes. I placed my cheeks against hers, held her gently as I could, without pressure, taking her excess of emotion into myself.

When I least expected it she said, "I cannot, must not live the way you want, but I'll think about how to come closer."

"We'll figure it out together."

She nodded. I nosed her hair aside from her neck, kissed her there, feeling her warm and specific against my lips. The walk back felt heavy with unspoken worries for both of us, but those could wait. We would feel our way

Mada

to the moment for talking and it would come. As we came around the last stand of trees on the road leading to the house, we saw the car at the same time and we knew this idyllic time had come to its end.

"Then let it happen," I said, pressing her hand. "Let it happen." I felt no fear, only a concern for Mada's well-being as we walked together towards the house. Fate had been kind in giving me this refuge and it still gave me strength. I could feel the peace and goddess-energy Mada and I had brought to it while we loved there. I didn't know what I would do or what would happen, but the comfort of those walls and Mada's presence made me unafraid.

It was good that I walked into it with such confidence because Ricard's face was hell to confront. It wasn't his anger; it was the sly evil behind the anger. I thought of Jake, an old-young man sitting among the boxes of strewn photographs. I thought of Mada's eyes that morning at the Cloisters and even earlier at our reunion in Central Park. I thought of Midge and that's where the thought began and ended.

I spoke first. "You didn't have her. You never had her."

Mada maybe didn't know what I was talking about, but it was between him and me now. His colour heightened by the cold, teeth long in his face, he knew immediately what I had and how much I knew. And I knew it all.

"You've been very industrious, my little Raquel."

"Cut the crap" I said. He sneered at my crude talk, but it stung him and he paled.

Mada

"How badly do you want to keep her young and healthy looking?" Referring to Mada as though she wasn't there was a mistake because she said, *"Niedertrachtig! Kuchenschabe!"* and even I caught the reference. But he was past words now. Maybe he had always been past them, the immaculate man wearing a civilized suit of clothes over a personal view of hell. Now only tatters linked him to the present. One of us would have broken the impasse, but just then the sound of another vehicle intruded as a compact with chains on its skinny tires came towards us in an icy skid that barely stopped short of the tarmac where we stood.

Rush was out of the car almost before it stopped and White followed him.

"Well," I said. "Did anybody remember to bring the marshmallows?"

CHAPTER 14

I THOUGHT WHITE MIGHT CRACK A SMILE, BUT HE KEPT A poker face. Rush, officious but for once not acting snide, ushered us into the house. I expected Ricard to leave but he didn't, White telling him, "Sorry, but we need you too."

For a moment it looked like Ricard would try to climb into his car anyway, but then his normal disdain returned and he said, "Of course, of course."

White and Rush flanked us and in we went, rather like lambs to the slaughter, but I told myself that I held the keys and I relaxed a little. Many people, three of them large men, filled my small living room. White told us to sit. He and Rush stood.

"We all know why we're here," said White.

"Why?" asked Mada. I regretted that she was the

Mada

only one in the dark, but I wasn't sorry about why I'd done it that way.

"Well, there are certain, ahem, materials," White began.

I hadn't expected him to get squeamish at the eleventh hour.

"They prove nothing," interjected Ricard.

Then I really began to wonder. "Aren't you," I asked, including both White and Rush in my gesture, "*his?*"

White grimaced and Rush said 'fuck' a few times under his breath.

"We understand your confusion, Miss Castellanos," White nodded meaningfully at Rush. "But to answer your question, our identities as presented to you are legitimate." They pulled out their ID's again in unison and flashed them.

"Wait a minute," said Ricard. His spit splattered in the air and White grimaced again.

"You can't be — you're not — you accepted money from me," Ricard protested.

"It's being held in evidence," said White.

"Too bad," sneered Rush.

"Yes. And you were verbally abusive to me and to her," I added, for a moment as confused as Ricard seemed. "Isn't that against Bureau policy?"

"We couldn't waste time," said Rush, but neither man apologized.

"Why should I believe you?"

"Yes, why?" said Mada, like an echo. White rolled his eyes at Rush.

"Look in the phone book, call the Bureau number for the State and ask for Department 872CP and verify our identities."

I did. They were legitimate.

"All right. What do you want?"

"What indeed?" said Ricard, trying to recoup his first hasty words.

"We'll deal with you later, sir," said Rush, the polite noun sounding strange from his mouth.

"As I said before, there are some materials," repeated White.

"How do I know we're talking about the same thing?" I said.

White looked pained, but he went on. "Certain negatives and photographs, a note, and a diary excerpt, all recovered by you in San Fran from goods belonging to Madeleine Tremaine."

Well, that was it, but I glanced at Ricard. He looked like he'd swallowed a large rock and it was lodged in his throat. It was slightly more than just a rhetorical question when I asked White, "Why should I give them to you? Maybe Ricard wants to trade?"

The hope flaring in Ricard's eyes was quickly squelched by Rush.

"That can't be allowed," he said with finality.

"Raquel, what's everyone talking about?" said Mada.

Mada

I went to my briefcase, took out Jake's note to Midge, put it on the table next to the one Mada had received. Mada drew in her breath. "So, that's what happened that night. My poor darling Midge," she said softly.

"Thanks to the two keepers of the flame, Jake and that one." I nodded towards Ricard, who curled his lip derisively. White and Rush did the same, as if to suggest we three women had gotten our just desserts, and Rush said, "Let's have the rest, Miss Castellanos." I put the two photos that had fallen from Mada's coat and sent me on the quest to San Francisco next to the calligraphic notes, then put two other photos beside them. Mada and I together. The tension in the room was almost palpable. Mada fixed Ricard with a look of pure contempt, Ricard practised his leer, and White and Rush stared at the photos with what they hoped to suggest was professional interest. Mada looked at me to confirm something.

"The two of them. Jake and Ricard."

"That was in the manila folder Midge had at Nepenthe," said Mada. It wasn't a question, but I answered her.

"It had to be. But you were right — later it made her do the best work of her life," I was speaking only to Mada now, as if no one else was there.

"She saw it there in the photos. She already had all the necessary elements, the artistic constructions, the intent — she just needed an idea of how to put it together. And when she got over being enraged and freaked out, she had it all."

Mada

I put down another photo besides the others. It was a working study in miniature, hand-coloured, black and white, of Mada, Midge and me, layered like the earth's history one upon the other and sketched in Midge's hand: the rose, the flower of life opening in the air above us, its roots taking its sustenance from our veins, red petals turned to the light. Midge had been the missing element, what we needed to give us dimension and substance, making us priestesses of time. The current flowing between Mada and I had taken us to another level in our relationship. An agreement only dimly understood before now emerged into clarity. It was as though Midge had been the conductor between us. We had only to see in the fusion our separate and real identities — to choose each other once again.

The moment released me and I saw Ricard, smug and complacent. Yet lurking in the back reaches of his eyes was a kind of stark fear. White, not completely mockingly, said, "This is obviously of importance to you."

"But let's get to the creamy centre — " said Rush, finally giving in to temptation, but White stopped him in mid-sentence, fastening me with a look that was half-challenging, half-expectant. "Okay," White said, "It's time to serve God and Country," and added, "you haven't showed us what we're looking for yet."

"The real stuff," Rush broke in again. White, however, had centred on me and wouldn't let go. I looked once more at Mada. Even with all the strain I saw the loveliness in her face. It seemed like her whole life lay in

Mada

her eyes: questioning and afraid. Mada, innocent, was unable to imagine Ricard's duplicity, knew White and Rush had stopped just short of drawing their guns and knew that would come too when they deemed it necessary.

Only Ricard's response eluded me — but I hadn't known White and Rush were for real. Now I knew they'd used all of us to zero in on their case, that they hadn't been above terrorizing Mada or using our feelings for each other to lead them to evidence they hadn't been able to find on their own. When had it started? Did they have a hand in Midge's death too? It wasn't that I didn't believe Ricard was guilty of everything they suspected, or that he didn't deserve to be punished; it was that I was being asked to choose one group of good ole boys over another, choose one part of an inhuman system over another. I was expected to make the choice without question because when women got to play in the male game, that was how it was done. To the victor the spoils? I didn't know what I was going to say until I said it.

"Midge was very clear about what she wanted done with her negatives, her photographs and her diary once either Mada or I saw it."

White cleared his throat and looked at Rush; the four of us looked at Ricard. His face had a crooked little smile starting at the corner of his mouth, but it stopped when I said, "She had it all, Ricard."

"Hand it over," Rush commanded.

I smiled to myself then shook my head. "Midge

Mada

wanted it all at the bottom of the Bay and . . ."

"You'll be arrested for destroying evidence, you'll be subpoenaed to testify against Mr. von Brecht, understand? And you'll be asked to describe your own sordid and lurid experiences in the company of both these people," White almost bayed.

"In detail," snorted Rush.

"I'm not guilty of anything," I retorted. "Midge's effects were disposed of as she wished. I have nothing to hide about my experiences with Mada and, furthermore, I've shown you everything."

"Raquel." I wasn't prepared for the anguish in Mada's voice. If I'd had the time to think it through, I might have known she'd react as she did.

"Mada, even if you don't understand right now, you have to trust me on this. Please." After a moment she nodded, but the pain and reproach stayed in her eyes, along with fear. That would have to wait, I told myself.

White and Rush exchanged looks and White took my arm and led me into the kitchen. He looked so alien in the company of the strudel Mada had made — obviously for my homecoming — and so awkward in the midst of the small signs of domesticity we had achieved.

"Listen," he said. "You might think you can deal with this on your own, but he could try to kill you and we won't be there to stop him." He stared at me hard then went on. "It's a multi-million dollar operation — you're like an ant he'll just squash."

I kept quiet. White finished, "He'll kill you both if he has to."

"He'd never hurt Mada," I said. She'd tried to make me believe that enough times.

"He drove Midge crazy and got her brother mixed up in it."

"But not Mada." I was trying to convince myself.

"Would you use her life as a pawn?" White asked. That hit hard and he knew it. He said soothingly, "Give us the evidence we need, Raquel, and she'll be safe. You'll both be safe."

I was weakening, but then he overplayed his hand. "You'll have your own life together, just the two of you," he said, as if he knew what that meant for Mada and me.

"There's nothing left." I said. "I threw it all in the Washboard." I was referring to the area under the bridge where the waters of the Bay meet those coming in from the open sea, creating fierce cross-currents that could grind anything to shreds in seconds.

White stared at me. I stared back. Finally he said, "Don't say I didn't warn you."

"No, I won't say that."

We went back into the other room where Mada sat stiffly on the sofa. Ricard was standing and so was Rush. White nodded to his partner and they went to the door together. After issuing various threats and warnings to each of us, they left. The door closed. Nobody moved or said anything. Our breathing and the gusting of the wind that had risen were the only sounds I heard.

Mada

It was Mada's call now. Our eyes met and I could see she understood what I had in mind. The temperature had dropped considerably and I could feel the bite so I set myself the task of building the fire. I put on my down jacket and snow-boots and went outside for the wood. Not even the south wall shielded me from the freezing wind — the windchill factor had to be five below Fahrenheit or worse. If more snow came on that wind, we'd be snow-bound for sure — not a pleasant prospect with Ricard in the house. Towards the north the sky was a massive grey shroud, the distant hills and forest already obscured by the advancing storm. I was carrying in several armloads of wood as the first flurries began to fall. The wind rose in sudden fury as I shut the outer door and began taking off my snow gear. I didn't hear voices inside so I opened the door and stepped in.

CHAPTER 15

Mada stood before the fire as though she'd been on her way somewhere and had stopped for a moment to watch the flames. Like the first time I had been alone with her, her magnetism made my knees weak. I wanted her to entice me all over again, so I could begin to surrender again. But Ricard was there, sitting with his legs crossed, one hand holding a cigarette, though it was unlit. The creases of his cashmere slacks were sharp and his shoe leather glowed. He had taken off his jacket to show gold cufflinks on French cuffs. Behind it all I saw the degraded bodies of children sold to unknown avenues of vice in red light districts across the world. When Mada turned to me the shadow of everything I knew about what had happened was in my eyes. She took it in and I started quietly and carefully to detail an elaborate scheme to free us both.

Mada

"If I hadn't gone to the lab to make a few prints for you, I never would have found it. When I opened the silver foil inside the box of photographic paper it was all there: the obscene letter, the negatives, the photos, some pages from her diary that gave the sequence of events or as much as Midge understood of what had happened."

Ricard began swinging his leg from side to side. His shoe clicked against the coffee table, drawing my attention, but Mada's eyes brought me back to her face. "When Midge got over being crazy, something about the letter alerted her and she traced it to Jake. Then she found out other things. Pretty soon she knew everything he did and more."

"My poor, darling Midge," Mada whispered again.

"Forget about that," I said, surprised by the bitterness I heard in my voice. Was my bitterness at Mada? Did I blame her for something? Because something wasn't quite right? I knew I'd put off telling Mada everything I knew for a reason — maybe it was because there was something I was afraid to find out.

As if she were listening to my thoughts Mada asked, "What were those two men talking about? What do they want?"

"Those uncouth jerks," Ricard broke in. "There's nothing for them to find out."

"They're after Midge's dairy. The names of contacts in the ghettos of New York and San Francisco," I went on. "Men who sell children to the degenerate markets of Europe. Ricard's men. Mada jumped at the sound of my

Mada

voice then turned to look at Ricard. I refused to be intimidated by the hatred in his face. He could not meet her eyes and stared only at me.

"Names, connections, dates, profit margins. How come you let Jake know so much?" I said to Ricard. Then I knew. "Or did he find out by himself? Jake wasn't so stupid after all, was he? He was covering his butt . . ."

"There's nothing to find," Ricard said. "No records, no personnel, no product. I have only legitimate businesses." Hence the smugness I had seen before in his face.

"There is one more thing," I said.

While they both watched me I picked up the phone and dialled the number I'd called earlier, got connected to Department 872CP again. This time a woman answered. She verified the physical descriptions I gave her of White and Rush and that they were working out of a San Francisco office. I'd checked out their badge numbers before, but this time I asked, "Rush needs his mouth washed out with soap, right?"

"Agent Rush is a born-again Christian," she countered. "He wouldn't be caught dead insulting the Lord."

I thought of the drawl that broke through White's careful language. "Is Agent White from Dixie?"

"Are you kidding?" she scoffed. "Brooklyn all the way."

Ricard had turned ashen. He crushed the unlit cigarette in a plate of walnuts.

"I guess that's all I need to know," I said and hung up.

Mada

I stood in front of the fire beside Mada, facing him. "When did you decide to get rid of Midge? After you found out what she knew?"

Again no answer. "It wasn't even about Mada, was it? Doing something so extreme out of jealousy would have been almost human. But no, that wasn't even it."

Mada's face was begging me to stop, but I had to say it all.

"It was only for business reasons," I told him. "You got rid of Midge because she knew about the business and you couldn't trust her not to tell Mada sooner or later. You pushed her towards her death as surely as if you had plunged the needle in yourself. And maybe you did."

The smear of self-pride on Ricard's face and the memory of Jake saying "bad drugs" told me I'd hit on the truth. Ricard threw back his head in a gesture I now recognised as utterly above it all.

Mada shook her head; maybe she didn't get it. "But how did she find the time?"

"In between the afternoon she spent with you and when she saw us both at Nepenthe she got the package from Ricard — the photographs — and then the truth or falsity of the letter ceased to have any weight. Maybe she convinced herself it was true after all."

"Ridiculous," said Ricard.

"In her own words," I said quietly, "she said it in her own words in her diary. You must have been ready to move, but that afternoon you were sure she knew and that was her ticket to Mada's freedom."

Mada

"That was the wonderful thing she was going to tell you," I said to Mada. "That you could be free, that there was enough on Ricard to put him out of your life forever, but when she saw the photographs of you and me together her worst nightmare came true. Once she finally sorted it all out we were gone from her life. And she couldn't ignore the fact anymore that her brother Jake was knee-deep in shit and that he would go down with Ricard. In spite of all this she came through for herself. Do you have any idea what that took?"

I guess I was throwing those words at the world. I was angry at Mada, at myself, for all we hadn't done for Midge. For how we'd left her to suffer, without extending ourselves. Angry at how events had contributed to making Midge a liability, one that Ricard couldn't allow. And I resented Mada for always playing for herself no matter the circumstances, resented her self-absorbed, dedication to her view of life, a dedication that had stopped being laudable at some point and became degenerate. I don't know when I started feeling that way. It had been there in the background ever since I'd read Midge's diary. That had been me back then too, and it had taken everything that had happened since then for me to see it.

Now my mind screamed out for retribution, but my heart tore itself in mourning. I saw in Mada's eyes her guilt and mine, and something else, forgiveness. But there was no time to express our feelings to each other. We were already full swing into an act that would risk our lives. We were improvising, cueing each other by tones and gestures, as

Mada

well as words known only to us. And we were holding up a mirror to reality for each other as well. After my phone call, Ricard knew for sure he couldn't get the information he thought I had. It had been a good play; I had almost fallen for it, but the effectiveness of Ricard's imposters, White and Rush, had ended. It was his move now.

While I waited I stood by the window, watching the snow fall. Silent substance of purity, absolving a cruel and undeserving world. I wanted to dance in its whirling brightness, free myself from all desire, from the truths taking me down.

And then he said it.

"There was nothing for Midge to tell Mada. Nothing she didn't know." Was the look on his face one of pity for me? For Midge?

"That's just what I'd expect you to say," I answered. My back to the window, I felt the cold snatching at me through the glass. He was eager for me to do as he asked.

"Look at her! Do you really think she turned her eyes away from business matters?" he went on. "That was just one more piece in her repertoire as an actress."

"Do as he says," Mada urged. "Look at me."

I did and the pain in those eyes made them a boiling sea.

Mada went on, "Yes, I suspected there was something. I chose not to know what."

"Your silence — "She finished my sentence."

— gave him the weapon he needed to attack Midge."

"Why?"

"Sins of omission are never easy to explain," she said.

"Please."

"I knew if I was seen to be mixed up in anything vile, I'd never work in front of an audience again."

"Why should your life be worth more than the lives of innocent, helpless children who were robbed of their futures each day you refused to know what Ricard was doing?"

"The evil in the world is much greater than I."

"That's not good enough. By choosing to protect yourself, you protected him and everything he did," I insisted.

"And now, Raquel, you know everything. You could have provided evidence against him, but you too have kept silent. Why?"

"At first I thought that if White and Rush had gotten to Jake it was probably already too late. Ricard would have already started to cover his tracks."

"What else?"

I let it fly. "Because you mean too much to me."

She drove it home mercilessly.

"Say it." she commanded, taking my face in her hand. I had to look into her eyes, feel her hands, smelling slightly of perfume, her touch so sensuous that I could neither deny nor resist her, though I suffered.

"Because of Midge. Because she wanted to protect you," I cried. I tried to pull away from her, but she held me, asking me with her eyes.

Mada

It came out in a moan. "Because of you. Because of us. If I forced you — dragged you through the scene that would have followed — it would have destroyed us. We would go on loving but would be unable to love, and I would have wanted to die and so would you."

Ricard was clapping in the background; he was really enjoying this. I turned on him. "What's the last thing *you* did for love, good or bad?" His face took on a know-it-all look.

"You were at the reading in Arizona, my little Raquel. You saw me with Mada, and you looked for me, pleaded with fate for me to find you and offer my wife to you."

"I counted on it. I would have consorted with demons just to see her." Somehow, speaking the truth made me stronger. "You knew me, I knew you, Mada and I knew each other, and we hid the truth. So now it's all out in the open at last: what we did for love. I was using you; you gave her to me. You thought I was the one you could control — do to me what you did to Midge. I know your kind of thirst to own and enslave. I have known it and put it aside. I won't be your avenging angel either. I won't play the system's dirty game for you."

In the heat of my exchange with Ricard, I had almost forgotten Mada, who now spoke. "Then give him what he wants, Raquel."

I hesitated. In the interval I heard the wind coming down from the high slopes and crashing against the north wall. I would take my stand in this house; alone and unresisting against the thrust of wind and snow. I guessed Ricard had to be bluffing about the business; the contacts must still be in place. He wouldn't be that eager to dismantle a worldwide network built up over a lifetime. Somewhere, someone could be made to talk, and Ricard knew it.

"Her or the business," I said. "You give Mada's history back to her. You give her whatever assets are hers — she knows what they are — and you let her go. Period."

I had put myself on the line and he made the move I was expecting. "I have no reason to bargain," he said as he pulled out the Luger he was carrying like an extra organ in the fold of his pants.

It didn't faze me. "Ricard, we both know that hurting me would finish you with Mada." For a second I wasn't sure I'd said the right thing, then the gun wavered and settled again, pointing at her.

If Mada was frightened or surprised she didn't show it. I was sorry to push him to that, but she had to know. I was holding my breath when she said, "Me or the business, Ricard."

Then I realized she meant she would trade herself to him. "Mada, you're not seriously considering . . . "

"I lived through the death of my family, of my country and of its rape by its conquerors. I'll survive this too."

"Forget it. First of all, there's no way you can trust him to do what he says. Secondly, I won't let you — not after how we've been with each other." A lopsided smile showed on her face, and it told me more than anything else had how much she cared about everything.

"Listen to me," I told her. "There's nothing he can do to me or to you that can stop the process already in place."

Above the howling of the wind I thought I heard something else. I went to the window and lifted the curtain but could see nothing on the road leading to the house. Whatever it was, it was raising the hairs on the back of my neck. The wind gusted again, and I put it down to the charged energy of the storm. Watching me, Ricard commanded me to explain my words.

"Just a little protection," I said, "in case there was no other way. Unless I make a phone call tonight, the whole mess is going to be on the feds' desk in the morning."

In the vacuum of disbelief that followed, I told Mada, "You don't have to sacrifice yourself."

"You're lying," said Ricard. "You've already said you won't hurt Mada."

I struggled. The words of our play were so mingled with bits of reality that it was easy. "It's better this way. With you she wouldn't have anything anyway."

"Raquel," Mada said, "let me do it my way." When I didn't answer her she said, "You can't decide my fate. You can't destroy my work, my life."

"Yours is only one life measured against the lives of many. You were right: there's no place for our love anymore. But I won't let you give yourself to him."

She tried to take my arm, but I pulled away. When she tried again I pushed her away. It was the first time I had touched her with anything but love in my hands, and my action was real enough to sear us both.

"I'd rather never see you again — I'd rather blow your life apart than let him touch you."

"Please, Raquel." The tears ran down her cheeks, but I turned away from them and looked instead at the room where we'd laughed and made love, the place I had hoped for a future with her. I backed up to the window again, feeling dead inside.

"There it is, Ricard: your freedom or Mada's freedom. Take your choice."

He'd been watching us intently, a peeping Tom spying on our emotions, caught like a fish, but I really didn't know which way he'd jump.

Then he said in icy tones, "I'll kill you both. Neither of you is worth as much as my work." Our expressions must have been something to behold because he looked at us and laughed, the laughter of a man who has embraced evil and now feels free to commit whatever cruelty he desires.

"Make your phone call, stupid," he told me. "Or I'll kill you now."

Now or later, I thought, but I picked up the phone like he told me to and dialled Susan's number in Stinsen Beach. He held the Luger next to my cheek, and I said, "It's okay, burn it."

"Just do it," I said to the question marks in her voice. I hung up the phone.

"And now you come with me," he told Mada.

Mada

"Never." He laughed some more. "Come, my dear, enough play acting." My heart pounded wildly, but he swung the gun towards me again and levelled it.

"I'll kill her now." So the feelings in our play were real enough to convince him after all, but he wielded the love we had for each other as a weapon: each would do anything to protect the other.

"As you said, my lovely Raquel, there's no room for you anymore."

So saying, he took the keys to the jeep and pushed Mada towards the door. This was the most dangerous moment: I had to trust her faith in me and her confidence in herself. But she went with him, and I saw her buttoning the overcoat I had given her as she climbed into the four by four.

Before the Mercedes had completely backed out to the road, I was racing to the rear of the house, buckling on my cross-country boots, grabbing the skiis and strapping a second pair on my back. I kept to the shadows along the hillside, tracking by sound. It was slow going, even for a four by four, because of the wind and poor visibility. But I knew the way blindfolded. I mentally patted myself on the back for those years of all-out races across the sand dunes on California beaches. I was light on muscle, because of weight loss, but my legs were like iron. I sidestepped up to the trees without a wasted motion and slid across the gulleys on the deer trail that would end three miles east at the river.

Two miles out, I got my second wind. The intense

cold and the windchill cut into my strength while the snow blinded me with its whiteness. Again I felt the unknown energy I had sensed at the window massing itself and raking its claws over the surface of the earth. I heard the Mercedes approaching the intersection by the river, the engine pausing before tackling the 45 degree angle uphill. I skimmed out of the trees in a flash, downhilled swiftly to the river and slid easily onto the ice.

I only had time to gauge distances and angles of retreat before the Mercedes crested the hill, hesitated for a split second, then bore directly down on me. The road curved ever so slightly, but Ricard didn't feel it — he was concentrating on me. Here, where the hillside partially sheltered the river, and the snow flattened the riverbanks, my bright red parka flashed like a beacon in a storm, pulling him beyond the safety of the road towards the snow-covered ice. He must have known then because I saw Mada struggle fiercely with him for the wheel as the car cartwheeled in a sideways skid towards the river. I shouted a few words of prayer to the Goddess for Mada before the engine revved high and the tires spun off the concealed riverbank. At the same time, I saw Mada leap from the car as its wheels hit the ice and it slammed like a listing ship, dead centre into the river.

I lost sight of Mada for a moment as I turned, retreating from the cracking ice. Huge jagged threads of ice split beneath my skiis, releasing the captive roar of the river from under the ice to eat the useless whining of the engine and spinning wheels. Even then Ricard might have saved himself if he had turned the wheel and allowed the winch to pull him backwards. But he didn't. He kept coming. I turned around, yelled at him to go back, but he answered me by pointing the Luger through the window and firing. I saw the flash as the ice burst apart. A thunderous cracking, splitting sound as the mighty force of the river swallowed the shot and spun the Mercedes around once before sucking it down into its maw like a stone. The last thing I saw was Ricard's red splotch of face from a distance in the second before he disappeared beneath the black, twisting waters.

Epilogue

It went down in the records as an accident, although the sight of Ricard's hand still clenched around the gun raised more than a few questions. Ricard's empire in the human flesh trade remained secret for the time being because Mada wanted it that way. Not for herself but because he had rescued her from East Berlin. She would make the final payment on that debt by seeing Ricard buried in the small Bavarian village of his boyhood without sullying his name. But the time would soon come when evidence of his foul work would be handed over to the proper authorities. We agreed on this after much soul-searching and we accepted the decision, knowing what it would cost. Perhaps it was the only way we could justify our happiness in each other.

Mada

The day before she left to take Ricard's body home, Mada and I went down to the river. The snow had stopped the next morning, and the scars and bruises left on the land by the investigating troopers were still fresh. Only the river had repaired itself, covering the wounds with ice and silencing the waters held in the grasp of winter. We stood in silence for a few minutes, each of us accepting our parts in all that had happened, including Midge's and Ricard's deaths. Then we walked hand-in-hand back to the house. When we parted at the airport she held my hands tightly as we looked into each other's eyes. We did it simply, without resistance, yet acknowledging the edge where our love had taken us. I waited until her plane left only a streak in the sky before I turned my back on the city and went home.

As the weeks went by new snows erased all signs of those awful minutes at the river. Often during the long frozen days of winter I turned to the fire as though its glow were Mada's, and I began to trace that strange unravelling of events, feelings and meanings. I have tried to write it all down, with all the self-deception and blindness we were all guilty of intact.

When it was time I closed the house and went to D.C. to finish my task at the Library of Congress. I returned to New York and in the calm that followed I outlined my research for the coming year. The day finally came when the buds began to open on the trees in Washington Square. Mada came back. We flew together to California.

Mada

As the sun rose over the wings Mada turned to me.

"Miene liebe, look." I didn't need to see where she pointed. I looked instead at her soft and generous mouth, into her green eyes. Our hands touched and all the beauty I needed to see was in her face.

Kleya Forté-Escamilla was born in border town of Calexico and grew up in Baja and in Arizona in a bi-cultural, bi-lingual family and environment. The writer of *Daughter of The Mountain*, Kleya's second book of ethnic work, *Nike Airs and the Barrio Stories,* will be published in 1994. Her short stories are in journals and anthologies, including, *Indivisible 2, anthology of Gay and Lesbian Writing of the West Coast,* and *Pieces of the Heart, New Chicago Writing,* edited by Gary Soto. Also a writer of Young Adult and Children's literature, her work appears in *Join In: Multi-Ethnic Stories for Young Adults* published by Bantam/Doubleday in the fall,1993.

She recently won the Astraea Foundation Award for writing – 1993.

She holds two BA degrees, one in French/Philosophy, one in Art, and an MA in writing. She is the mother of one son.